# THE MIZZY MYSTERIES

## A SKELETON IN THE CLOSET

FOR EVERY CHILD WHO LONGS TO BE SEEN
FOR WHO THEY REALLY ARE... —CH-S

Text copyright © 2025 by Claire Hatcher-Smith
Cover art copyright © 2025 by Robyn Kearns
Family Tree illustrations and "Lester Upper" type face
copyright © 2025 by Lester Magoogan
Illustration taken from *The Mizzy Mysteries — A Skeleton in the Closet*
published by Farshore 2025

Tundra Books, an imprint of Tundra Book Group,
a division of Penguin Random House Canada Ltd.,
320 Front Street West, Suite 1400, Toronto, Ontario, M5V 3B6, Canada
penguinrandomhouse.ca

Published simultaneously in the United States of America by Tundra Books of Northern New York, an imprint of Tundra Book Group, a division of Penguin Random House Canada Ltd., P.O. Box 2040, Plattsburgh, NY 12901, USA

Tundra with colophon is a registered trademark of
Penguin Random House Canada Ltd.

All rights reserved. No part of this book may be reproduced, scanned, transmitted, or distributed in any form or by any electronic or mechanical means, including information storage and retrieval systems, without permission in writing from the publisher, except by a reviewer, who may quote brief passages in a review. No part of this book may be used or reproduced in any manner for the purpose of training artificial intelligence technologies or systems.

The authorized representative in the EU for product safety and compliance is
Penguin Random House Ireland, Morrison Chambers, 32 Nassau Street,
Dublin D02 YH68, Ireland, https://eu-contact.penguin.ie

Publisher's note: This book is a work of fiction. Names, characters, places and incidents either are the product of the author's imagination or are used fictitiously, and any resemblance to actual persons living or dead, events, or locales is entirely coincidental.

Library and Archives Canada Cataloguing in Publication

Title: A skeleton in the closet / Claire Hatcher-Smith.
Names: Hatcher-Smith, Claire, author.
Description: Series statement: The Mizzy mysteries ; 1
Identifiers: Canadiana (print) 2024041196X | Canadiana (ebook) 20240412036 | ISBN 9781774885116 (hardcover) | ISBN 9781774885123 (EPUB)
Subjects: LCGFT: Detective and mystery fiction. | LCGFT: Novels.
Classification: LCC PS8615.A78198 S54 2025 | DDC jC813/.6—dc23

Library of Congress Control Number: 2024940743

Cover designed by Gigi Lau
Production edited by Bharti Bedi
The text was set in Georgia.

Printed in Canada

1 2 3 4 5     29 28 27 26 25

CLAIRE HATCHER-SMITH

# THE MIZZY MYSTERIES

## A SKELETON IN THE CLOSET

tundra

# MY FAMILY

NEFFUE

GRATE ANT JANE
(DED)

GRATE ANT ROZE
(REELLEE OLD)

GRATE UNKEL RAYMUND
(REELLEE OLD)

ANTY G
(LUVLEE)

UNKEL DAYVID
(OLDISH)

UNKEL LIYONELL
(OLDISH)

NIKO (16)   OLI (13)   CHERREE SUMBODEE
(NOT FAMILY)

# TREE

BY ME (MIZZY) 12 3/4 YRS

— NEECE

GRAMPA JONNEE   GRANMA MABEL
(DED)           (ANCHENT)

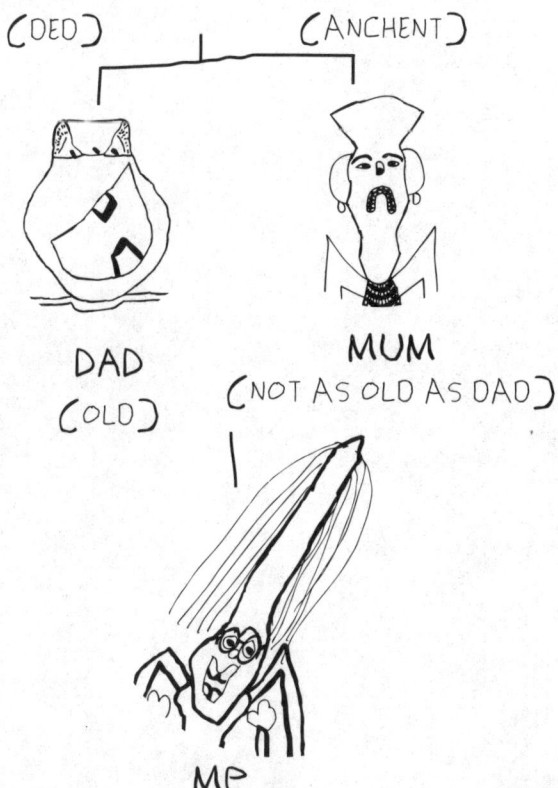

DAD        MUM
(OLD)   (NOT AS OLD AS DAD)

ME
12 3/4 YRS

# ONE

# The Case of the Swapped Swimsuit

Call me Mizzy, everybody does.

Actually, my cousins call me Miz (or Misery when I'm really annoying) but in my head, I'm Mizzy the Marvelous, world-famous detective. Think Sherlock Holmes crossed with Rachel Bailey, the police detective from that old show *Scott and Bailey* – the one with big brown eyes, never-ending legs and long, elegant fingers. Sometimes I want to be her so much, it hurts.

You see, I've wanted to be a detective for as long as I can remember. It's in my blood, or something. My cousins say I can sniff a mystery no one else has even noticed and my tummy just has a knack for feeling things.

They're right. My tummy fizzes at the first sign of a

secret. Sometimes it tightens into a small, hard lump as well. Sometimes it loops and tumbles and twirls.

What I'm not so good at yet is actually solving things. Mum and Dad just roll their eyes and say my dreams are Great Aunt Jane's fault and could I please stop poking my nose into other people's business already?

But I can't help it. And one day, they'll see. One day, I'll show them I'm a proper detective. I'll make them proud.

Maybe today's the day. After Sunday lunch with Grandma Mabel, we've made our way to the ponds on Hampstead Heath. Mum and Dad whisper a bit more about pork and porridge for lunch *again* and how maybe it's time to find Grandma Mabel a nice care home. Then we leave Dad at the Floaty-Boat Pond and Mum, Grandma Mabel and I head to the Ladies' Pond for my swimming lesson.

Like every summer Sunday, the pond and the dock and the grass are filled with families. Mums and grandmas and girls of all ages. Almost-grown-up ones in bikinis stretched out on towels in the sun. Littlies in frilled swimsuits and rubber rings and water wings. And groups of almost-teenagers, like me, hanging their legs off the end of the dock and giggling.

Except they're not like me, are they?

I tug at the frill on my swimsuit. Mum says it's cute, but almost-teenagers aren't supposed to be cute. We're meant to be cool. Like that girl over there with the swim shorts and crop top. I bet her mum even lets her wear lip gloss.

And that one over there, she's wearing mascara. There's streaks of it running down her face.

And not a single other twelve-and-three-quarters-year-old wears water wings.

My cheeks sizzle. I should be pulling on the darn things but, like always seems to happen right about now, something much more interesting catches my eye.

Today, a woman with a shark tattoo on her left wrist strolls up to a gray-haired lady a few towels away from me who's fast asleep on the dock. (I can tell she's sleeping, because her tummy goes up and down exactly the same amount with each breath and her snores drown out the bees zigzagging in the reeds.)

Shark-Wrist pauses a moment. Then, cool as the ice-cream cone Dad always promises me if I actually manage to swim, she slips her hand in Snory-Gray-Hair's bag and pulls out a navy-and-white-striped swimsuit. She holds the suit up to the light, like she doesn't want to steal a holey one, then strolls back along the dock to the changing room.

Is Shark-Wrist stealing the swimsuit? My heart hops. This is my next case. The one that'll show Mum and Dad I'm a proper detective. That'll show them I should wear lip gloss and a crop-top bikini and forget all about water wings.

Mum is digging around in our bag. She hasn't noticed a thing. Tummy fizzing, I scramble to my feet and, ever-so-cool-and-Rachel-Bailey-like, saunter after Shark-Wrist.

Outside the changing room, I stop and study the flaking rubber safety ring on the wall, like I'm fascinated by flaky, rubbery things. (Rachel Bailey calls this *surveilling*.)

Fourteen (well-examined) rubbery flakes later, Shark-Wrist reappears through the changing-room door. Wearing the swiped-striped swimsuit.

My heart thumps faster. I'm going to catch a real thief! A gazillion shades of lip gloss tumble through my head. Mum will be so proud. I stumble after Shark-Wrist and as she reaches the end of the dock where the wood pokes out over the water, I grab her arm and yell, "Gotcha!"

"Excuse me?" Shark-Wrist swivels and peers down at me, forehead all sorts of wrinkly. But her eyes don't flick from side to side. Her face doesn't turn red.

Oops. My tummy tightens. Have I got the wrong end of the stick?

"Mizzy!" Mum appears from nowhere. "Let go of the lady. At once."

My lip-gloss dreams vanish. "But, Mum . . . the swimsuit! It isn't hers!"

"Right now." Mum gives me one of her best glares,

then turns to Shark-Wrist. "I'm so sorry. She likes to make things up."

I hang my head.

But Shark-Wrist smiles down at me. "She's right, actually. It isn't my swimsuit."

It isn't? I sneak a glance at Mum.

"Mine had a hole in it," Shark-Wrist continues. "So I swapped with my aunt."

Then she nods at Snory-Gray-Hair, pats my head and dives into the pond.

# TWO

# The Saver

My cheeks burn. Another failure. A swapped swimsuit, not a swiped one. Rachel Bailey shakes her head. I should have surveilled a bit longer.

Mum obviously wishes I hadn't surveilled at all. Giving me one of her best why-do-you-poke-your-nose-in-where-it's-not-needed sighs and squeezing my fingers a bit too tight, she drags me back along the dock to our pile of swimming bags. "That's quite enough Great-Aunt-Janeing for today."

Great Aunt Jane is actually my great *great* aunt but that takes too long to say. She's famous in our family for being terribly nosy, watching all the neighbors and writing down stories about them in her diaries. Depending on who you ask (her nephew, Great Uncle Raymond, or her niece, Grandma Mabel), she was either an interfering busybody with a talent for getting the wrong end of the stick, or a *brilliantly* perceptive surveiller. It's a shame that all of her old diaries went missing years ago, because I'd love to read them.

Anyway, the only thing everyone agrees on is that I'm just like her.

I sigh. I'd rather be like Rachel Bailey, not a very-dead, very-nosy great aunt. But my eyes are blue and squinty, my legs are short, and my fingers are always sticky, even when I haven't eaten anything. And although my tummy usually knows when something's up, it never shares any actual facts with my brain.

To be absolutely honest, I haven't ever solved a real case. The closest I get is playing our Sherlock and Two Watsons game with my cousins, and even then, I'm a Watson.

Mum finishes rummaging through our swimming bags and pulls out my half-inflated water wings. Then grabbing each wrist in turn (much harder, by the way, than I grabbed Shark-Wrist's), she rams them up my arms.

Mum blows and puffs and blows some more and the wings pinch and squeeze my arms like two tubes of toothpaste. I close my eyes. The other almost-teenagers will be pointing at me and snickering, I'm sure of it.

"Hop in the water quick," Mum says, "before Grandma Mabel forgets what she's waiting for." Her voice has that tight, worried sound it always has these days when she talks about Grandma Mabel.

In the middle of the pond, Grandma Mabel's sun hat bobs up and down, like a giant yellow butterfly. Waiting for me. Encouraging me. I gaze at the pond and sigh. There's no way out. Even someone smuggling the Crown Jewels away in a wet towel won't budge Mum's eyes off me, not after my performance with Shark-Wrist.

I plonk down on the dock and lower my feet into the pond. My toes wobble like worms in the sunlit water. Teensy fish flick around my ankles in flashes of silver and green.

If only I could stay right here, like this. But Mum says swimming is a vital life skill and I have to learn it. And the kids at school say that even babies know how to swim.

A dragonfly zigzags across the surface of the water. A blackbird whistles in the roses.

Like a slowed-down video (or a really bad dream), Grandma Mabel stretches her arms toward me.

My tummy plummets. I tug at my water wings. I tug at the bottom of my swimsuit. Sprawled on the dock, a gazillion almost-teenagers turn in my direction. *Today, finally, will the beached-baby-whale-in-the-bubblegum-pink-water-wings-the-size-of-Battersea-Power-Station actually swim?*

"It's your last chance, Mizzy." Mum dips a toe in the water and kicks a little my way. "There won't be any swimming opportunities with your cousins in St. Jude's Junction."

I sigh. Of course there won't. That's one of the reasons I love it there.

Grandma Mabel smiles and waves.

My teeth start to chatter. The lump in my throat swells to the size of my water wings. But taking a deep breath of pond-scented air, I grit my teeth, swallow the lump in my throat and launch myself into the water.

So what if other almost-thirteen-year-olds don't need water wings? So what if my drowning-doggy-paddle sends ducks flapping for their lives? I can do it. I can still make Mum and Dad proud of me.

And what do you know, I AM doing it! I'm actually swimming! Away from the reeds. Past the end of the dock. Out into the deep water.

The deep water! My arms freeze. My legs melt. My heart stops. Weeds grab my ankles. Sloopy ice floods my nose. Darkness tugs at my toes.

And all at once, like it does every week, a birdlike arm loops my neck and Grandma Mabel tows me back to the reeds.

"I wasn't scared." I scrabble onto the dock and gasp for breath. "I just don't like water in my ears."

Mum smiles her there-there-baby smile. "Maybe next time, darling. It'll be September before you know it."

My bottom lip wobbles. So much for Mizzy the Marvelous.

"Never mind, dear." Grandma Mabel peeks out from under her floppy yellow hat and pats one of my water wings. "I'll always save you."

I sigh. Doesn't anybody understand? Mizzy the Marvelous doesn't need to be saved.

Mizzy the Marvelous is the saver.

## THREE

# Escalators

We collect Dad from the Floaty-Boat Pond, then make our way back across the heath.

Grandma Mabel somehow manages to stride ahead, even though she's tiny. Between her floppy hat and her floaty dress, all that shows are her itty-bitty feet. Her shabby white tennis shoes with frilly socks (scissored at the ankle so they're not too tight) scurry ahead of us through the woods.

Mum and Dad take the chance to hiss about Grandma Mabel getting forgetful and isn't it time to talk about care homes again? At least I'm not the only member of the family being babied these days. But it doesn't help much. My hair drips pond water down the back of my T-shirt and I shiver. Not just because I'm wet.

I didn't solve a crime again, did I? I didn't manage to swim. Again. The kids at school are right. I am a baby.

At last, we pass the final pond, the trees thin and the wide, grassy slope of the heath opens out around us. Sunshine. Families. Yapping dogs and Frisbees. And the ice-cream van. Mum shakes her head, but Dad buys me a cone anyway (even though I still didn't swim).

I snuggle up beside him on the prickly grass. London shimmers below our stretched-out feet and I lick a big, fat tongueful. This is one of my favorite parts of the week. But today the Shard twinkles in the distance, like it's showing off how grown-up and marvelous it is. Not like me.

My ice cream clogs at the back of my throat. What I need is a proper mystery. With impossible clues that no one else can solve, except me. I'll find the culprit and everyone will be amazed and they'll wonder how they never noticed how incredibly grown-up and marvelous I am (and don't I look like that tall, willowy detective on TV . . . what's her name again?).

But where on earth do I find a mystery like that?

The following day, like the baby I am, Mum and Dad deliver me and my My Little Pony suitcase to Victoria train station, to catch the train to St. Jude's Junction.

I spend almost every school holiday in St. Jude's with my cousins, because Mum and Dad are nurses and work different shifts at the hospital and almost-thirteen-year-olds can't be left on their own at home (even though technically they're not alone, because one of their parents is upstairs sleeping).

Don't get me wrong. Mum and Dad come down to see me on their days off, so I'm not a total orphan. And St. Jude's Junction is my favorite place in the whole world and my cousins are my most favorite people in it. I'm just not so keen on the not-being-old-enough-to-be-left-alone part, or the Victoria station part.

I'm especially not keen on the Underground.

As usual, we joined the Tube at Putney Bridge, a nice above-ground Underground station with lovely, low, very-not-moving staircases. But Victoria is a whole different disaster.

As our tube train pulls into the platform, people surge around us, out of the carriage, into the tomb-like tunnel and on through the archway toward the escalators. Like a mega-millipede that knows exactly where it's going and never gets lost and that isn't scared of anything.

Especially not escalators.

I wobble across the gap between the train and the edge of the platform, then my feet refuse to budge another step. Voices clang in my ears. The filthy, greasy smell of the Underground catches at the back of my throat and my mind floods with memories. Escalators. Tap-dancing at the top or bottom, while half of London lines up behind me. Clutching the handrail so hard, my feet get left behind me. The stomach-churning upside-downing. Stop buttons pressed (Mum) and wailing babies (me) being carried up or down the unmoving-moving staircase.

But we never use the escalators, of course we don't. Not anymore. Holding tightly to one hand each, Mum and Dad half lead, half carry me along the platform in the opposite direction to the millipede, away from the archway, toward the safety of the elevator.

I can just about breathe again. Victoria station has elevators for all its different tube lines and we haven't had to use an escalator in years. A few more minutes and I'll be on the train to St. Jude's. But when we reach the elevator at the end of the platform, it's out of order.

We stand and stare at the big black letters, like maybe if we look hard enough for long enough, they'll say something different.

Mum gives up first. "How can it be out of order? It's practically brand-new." She checks her watch. "Your train leaves in eight minutes." She bites her lip. Glances at Dad. "We'll have to use the escalator."

"No . . ." My tummy plummets. My knees wobble. Barf coats the back of my throat.

"Now, Mizzy." Mum squeezes my hand. "Take some breaths. We've got you."

Dad squeezes my other hand. "It's OK, love. We're here."

"But . . ." But what? I can't? I'm scared? I'm too much of a baby? Isn't that what I'm trying to show Mum and Dad I'm not? Well, Mizzy the Marvelous, here's your chance.

The mega-millipede has vanished and apart from a rumpled newspaper, a chewed-up wad of gum and a scrunched bag of cheese and onion chips, the platform is empty. I swallow my mouthful of barf, shake my hands free and, sneakers squeaking on the tiled floor, I stride ahead of Mum and Dad back toward the archway.

The escalator rumbles in the distance. It grumbles. It groans. With chattering teeth, I force one foot in front of the other. Closer. Closer. Closer. Until the towering metal monster rears up above me.

The ground shakes. My tummy churns. Another surge of barf fills my mouth. But squeezing my eyes tight shut, I hold my breath and launch myself on board.

And suddenly, I'm doing it. I'm on the escalator.

Going up, up, up.

Then all at once, I'm not doing it.

The top half of me starts to go down. I grab for the handrail and my feet carry on without me, up, up, up, while my head and shoulders and tummy go down, down, down. I gasp for air and screams I really ought to recognize bounce off the echoing walls.

I'm almost completely upside down when there's a juddering clank and the escalator freezes.

Dad scoops me into his arms.

And along with my My Little Pony suitcase, the biggest baby in the world is carried to the top.

# FOUR

# St. Jude's Junction

You're probably wondering how on earth Mum and Dad ever let me travel this last leg to St. Jude's Junction on my own, right? But they hand-deliver me onto the train at Victoria and Uncle David yanks me off at the other end. And, for the in-between part, Dad hisses all kinds of warnings in the conductor's ear and Mum makes me swear to follow her rules (don't talk to strangers, don't make up stories about them and definitely don't accuse them of stealing things they've swapped, or borrowed, or been given as a true and properly permitted sort of present). Really, the way they flap and fuss making "arrangements" for me, you'd think people with Down syndrome aren't capable of anything.

I'm sorry, I thought I mentioned the Down syndrome thing. It's not like I can hide it – my extra chromosome comes with a whole bunch of other stuff. A hole in my heart. A too-fat tongue. Sideways creases on the palms of my hands. Not to mention this really weird gap between the first two toes on each foot (which I didn't know was weird, until Judy Mitcham pointed at my feet in gym class and burst out laughing).

The most annoying thing is that people think we're all the same. We're not. We're not always happy. We don't love everybody (I hate Judy Mitcham). And we're not helpless, half-witted babies, who need to wear giant bubblegum-pink water wings, be bought consolation ice-cream cones and be carried up (and down) escalators.

OK, so that last part might be true for me. But other than escalators, swimming and bus routes (and did I mention I'm terrified of buttons?), I can do pretty much everything everyone else can. But whatever I do – however clever or funny or just plain normal I am – people always add the *for someone with Down syndrome* part.

The only people who don't treat me like I'm special for all the wrong reasons are my cousins Niko and Oli. Niko is the oldest. He turned sixteen in June, so he's always in charge, but he's really good at coming up with games to play, so we don't mind too much. Oli is only three weeks older than me, so we're practically twins and neither of us gets to boss the other one around. Most important of all, neither Niko nor Oli ever treat me like a baby.

As my train pulls out of Victoria station, and escalators and being carried and Mum and Dad and their flappy waving-at-the-baby hands disappear from view, I settle back in my fuzzy orange seat and smile.

Finally. Six whole weeks in my most favorite place, with my most favorite people ever. We'll play Clue and murder in the dark and our Sherlock and Two Watsons game.

I'll be Mizzy the Marvelous again.

An hour later, Uncle David meets my train. The station is in the middle of nowhere and the ten-minute drive to St. Jude's Junction always feels like forever. But eventually the village comes into view, folded in among the fields. First the main street fringed with whitewashed cottages, each with a different-color front door. Then the butcher's and the baker's and the teeny little supermarket that sells only tins of things. Then the village green and the pub. Then the church. Until, finally, Church Lane with its little stone walls and waterfalls of roses leads us to Auntie G's house.

Number One Church Lane used to belong to Great Aunt Jane. It's even more ancient than she was. She gave it to her nephew, Great Uncle Raymond, when she died. Great Uncle Raymond gave it to his son Uncle David and David's wife, Auntie G, ages ago, when Great Uncle Raymond bought an enormous new house on the other side of the village. Niko and Oli are Uncle David and Auntie G's kids. My cousins.

Number One is a crumbly, red-brick cottage on the end of a row of neat, whitewashed ones. Oli says the neighbors don't like its crumbliness, or the overgrown garden, or the thatched roof that looks like a lopsided wig. (And Niko says they're never invited in to comment on the creaking floorboards in the hall that dip in the middle, or the teeny windows that make the rooms all dark and stuffy, or the sweet, spicy smell from those seeds Auntie G crunches up for her coffee.)

But I think it's perfect, just like Auntie G. It's comfy and it doesn't try to be something it isn't and it's always ready to hug me as I am (which today means Starbucks-sticky from the train).

I leap out of the car, weave my way through the roses and the floppy, flouncy poppies and, tummy fizzing, race up the front path. I can't wait to pick up Sherlock and Two Watsons where we left off at Easter – partway through a particularly gruesome hatchet case, all evidence pointing to the vicar's son. But as my fingers fumble with the doorknob, the door flies open and Niko breezes past me on the step.

"Oh, hi, Miz." Niko's always been Sherlock. But today, he pats my head, pulls his hood over his (new) pink hair and lopes off down the front path.

My mouth drops open. He's never patted my head before. And we usually launch straight into the game. But Niko's halfway down the street, past the church already. He doesn't look back once.

The neighbors look though. Miss Batt, next door, peeks through her lace curtains. Mr. Belfry stops mowing the churchyard and lowers his glasses to get a better view. Even the robin in Auntie G's roses stops singing and cocks his head as he stares me up and down.

I close my mouth. I shouldn't mind – somebody arriving from anywhere is a big deal in St. Jude's – but today my cheeks are blazing. Did they see the pat on the head?

Lifting my chin, I saunter through the door and try to look like being babied on doorsteps by beloved cousins is my favorite summer holiday thing to do. Uncle David drags my suitcase up the path, rolls his eyes and mutters something about teenagers. I roll mine back, to show I don't care. Then I set off in search of Oli.

Niko might have spent the last four months turning into a cool, pink-haired stranger (who pats me on the head), but Oli will be as excited to play the game as I am. I can't wait till he hears my brilliant theory about the vicar's son.

Oli's in the kitchen, leaning against the counter, cramming an entire slice of pizza in his mouth. My heart always goes sort of mushy when I first see him again, but today a pineapple tang catches at the back of my throat and my heart puddles around my ankles.

At Easter we were pretty much the same height. Now Oli towers over me. And he has brand-new cheekbones to boot.

"Hi, Miz," he says, his voice all deep and different and not just because his mouth is full. "Mum said to tell you she's at the greyhound shelter." He wipes his sleeve across his face, reaches for another slice of pizza and balances a soccer ball on one enormous foot, all at the same time (rather impressive, actually). "I'm to give you your tea and find you something to watch till she gets back. Dad's working from home now, in your old room. So you're upstairs," he adds, like he's reading from a list. "In the creepy spare room, poor you. I've got practice at six."

I check the kitchen clock (the one with Flower Fairies instead of numbers) and my heart-puddle seeps across the floor. Soccer practice is in five minutes. No time to share my theory. Or to tell Oli we only need one Watson and I'm happy to be Sherlock. No time for anything.

As if to prove my point, Oli grabs another piece of pizza, then dribbles his soccer ball across the kitchen, along the hall and out through the front door.

Gone.

I swallow the lump in my throat. Niko is one thing (he is older, after all), but Oli too? In case you hadn't noticed, he's my favorite. We always do everything together.

But now he prefers soccer?

I swallow the rest of the pizza – stuffed-crust, Hawaiian (not my favorite, but you know). Then I slump on the sofa and watch old episodes of *Scott and Bailey* and wait for Auntie G to come home. At least *she'll* be pleased to see me.

But, in keeping with the rest of my evening, Auntie G doesn't come home. Neither do either of the boys. Uncle David appears from his room (my room) and joins me for half an episode, but if you've met Uncle David you'll know he doesn't count. (If you haven't met him, think one-word sentences, mostly about trains.)

So much for my wonderful summer.

It's just Uncle David, *Scott and Bailey* and me.

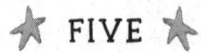

# FIVE

# The Case of the Locked Wardrobe

When Uncle David slopes back to his office, I turn off the TV and drag myself upstairs. It isn't quite bedtime yet, but I might as well check out my new room.

*You're upstairs in the creepy spare room, poor you.*

Poor me is right. As I open the spare-room door, warm air wraps around me like an unwanted hug from a little old lady, stale and sickly sweet. I should be tucked up downstairs in my old room, with hot chocolate and Oli and Niko on the end of my duvet, playing bedtime Clue and planning tomorrow's Sherlock game. But they're both long gone.

The wallpaper's a peeling tangle of grayish rosebuds and the whole tiny space is crammed to the ceiling with old-lady furniture. The sort Grandma Mabel loves and I hate – too big and too dark and taking up too much space. To top things off, half of the floor and the dressing table are piled with boxes and jars and plastic shopping bags stuffed with who-knows-what. *Everything* is coated with dust.

The floorboards creak as I pick my way across the threadbare carpet to the bed. The springs squeak and dust puffs up around me. I perch beside my suitcase (thoughtfully dumped upside down by Uncle David) and do my best to ignore the washed-out bedspread that's scratching the back of my legs where my leggings and socks don't reach.

My sigh fluffs my bangs and I sniff. My room downstairs was always lemony-clean. Uncle David's desk took up all of one wall and I had to sleep on a sofa bed, but for the school holidays at least, with my very own My Little Pony duvet and a stack of Flower Fairies books beside my pillow, Auntie G made it feel like mine.

But this room is a dumping ground. For unwanted, grown-out-of stuff.

Like baby cousins.

Back home, I taped a chart to my bedroom wall and crossed off the days till I'd be back in my most favorite place in the whole wide world. But Niko is off doing teenager things, Oli has soccer and even Auntie G seems to prefer greyhounds this summer.

What's a favorite place without the favorite people? The rosebud wallpaper wobbles and blurs and, less Mizzy the

Marvelous, more Mizzy the Making-Do, I heave my suitcase the right way up and start to unpack.

My spirits lift a little. On top of my leggings and T-shirts and socks are two prettily wrapped parcels. Roses and ribbons and my name printed on top of each one. It's Mum's writing, but one present is from her and Dad and one says it's from Grandma Mabel.

Fingers fumbling, I open Mum and Dad's one first. Great. Another journal. Of course. I drop the book (and the paper and the ribbon) like it's dog poo. Every holiday it's the same thing. This journal is shimmery pink, with a padded silver unicorn and huge gold letters on the front, yelling *MY AMAZING LIFE* at me. Another of Mum's not-so-cunning tricks to get me to practice my spelling.

I frown. Neither my life nor my spelling are very amazing (yet) and I'm definitely not going to write down any innermost thoughts, just so Mum can read them and check up on my handwriting.

I turn to Grandma Mabel's present. It's long and thin and I've been dropping hints about makeup for ages, so it's probably one of those multipacks of eyeshadows or lip glosses. There might even be blusher in there too, to make my cheeks more Rachel-Bailey-hollow-looking. I pull at the bow, tear off a pleasing sweep of paper and peek inside.

Eyeliners?

My tummy fizzes. So many colors! Every possible shade I could ever want!

But hang on a minute . . .

As I yank the plastic packet out of the paper, my tummy flumps. These aren't eyeliners. They're markers. Pip-Squeaks Skinnies, true – but markers all the same.

Grandma Mabel and I used to color every Sunday afternoon, after swimming. She saved cartoons from the newspaper and bought books of those pretty-pattern things (mandolins or something) and the pictures you have to solve by connecting all the dots. But that was ages and ages ago. Like everything else these days, Grandma Mabel's forgotten how old I am.

I toss the packet on the floor beside Mum's journal and turn to the rest of my unpacking. There isn't much room, but the top drawer of the dressing table is empty (the bottom two are wedged tight with lavender bags and old sweaters). I stuff in my underwear and socks and leggings and T-shirts. It's a tight fit, but luckily all my clothes are soft and stretchy (with absolutely no buttons).

All that's left to unpack is my new dress. In spite of the spare room, in spite of no cousins, no detective games and babyish presents, I smile.

Grandma Mabel turns eighty next weekend and there's going to be a party on Saturday, here at Auntie G's. Everyone will come, including Mum and Dad. Mum even let me choose a special dress for the occasion all by myself, so it doesn't have buttons, or frills, or flowers, or bows. My heart swells all over again as I pull it from the case.

This is a Rachel Bailey dress. It's long and smooth and midnight blue all over and I feel beautiful and brave and ever-so-clever-at-solving-things when I wear it. When I tried it on in the shop, Mum frowned and Dad got a bit teary (which either means it was too much money, or too grown-up). But they bought it for me anyway.

I drape the silk over my arm and stroke away the creases. Then I pick my way across the carpet, through the boxes and the shopping bags to the wardrobe. This dress shouldn't be crammed in a drawer.

But when I try to open the wardrobe door, it's stuck fast.

I yank and pull and tug, but the door won't budge. It's probably just stuffed with junk and locked so the boxes and plastic bags don't tumble out.

But (my heart risks a little hop) what if it isn't?

A locked wardrobe. I bend down and peer through the dark keyhole. Maybe it's just the shut-up smells of the spare room or the lavender bags – but for the first time since I arrived at Auntie G's, there's a teensy whiff of mystery in the air.

Rachel Bailey peeks over my shoulder. What if there isn't junk inside the wardrobe? What if there's something else?

Rachel Bailey raises one eyebrow. Mizzy the Marvelous tries to do the same. We both smile.

We need to get ourselves inside.

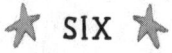

## Inside the Wardrobe

The wardrobe is massive. Ceiling-high, with towering, curved corners, a door as tall as Oli and ginormous carved claws on the bottom. Like a crouched lion, or a hideous hound.

Behind the mottled mirror on the door there might be jagged teeth.

There might be a belly full of bones. An actual skeleton in a closet.

It's all I can do not to twirl around the room with excitement. But then swiped-striped swimsuits float before my eyes.

I'm getting ahead of myself. First, I need to check for a key.

Laying my dress carefully on the bed, I surveil the room in my most-best-Bailey style. I check the rims of the two pictures on the wall – an old steam train and, for some reason, three blindfolded mice. My fingers collect a thick sweep of dust, but no key. No key behind the pictures either. Or inside the frames.

I wipe my fingers on my leggings. Best check the floor next. I pick each box and plastic bag from the pile on the floor and rummage through their contents. Balls of wool, lumpy cardigans, newspapers and magazines tumble to the floor. Shortly joined by soaps (the sickly-sweet smell!), chocolate digestive cookies (the stale smell!) and cans of something called *Spam*.

But still no key.

I bite my lip, but Bailey nods at the bed. I pick my way across the carpet, lift the bedspread from the floor and peer underneath. I even shine the light from my phone, just to be sure. But there's only more dust, two dead moths and a spider (very much alive).

The only place left to look is the dressing table. The top drawer is now crammed with my stuff, but this time, I make a proper investigation of the bottom two drawers. Among the old sweaters are old stinky balls of something to protect the clothes, little paper bags leaking crumbled lavender, and old stamps ripped off envelopes, faded and yellowed at the edges. Still no key. But I do find a magnifying glass, shoved in the back corner of the very bottom drawer. I place it on the bed with my dress and flump down beside it.

The room now looks like an exploded rummage sale. Never mind a needle in a haystack, this is like hunting for the midge that bit me at the Ladies' Pond.

Except . . . Hang on a minute. What's that you're saying, Bailey? Of course! The *top* of the dressing table. I've checked the drawers, but I haven't looked properly at the junk on top.

Back at the dressing table, I run my hand around the mirror. And behind it. I lift the corner of each lacy mat, check the can of mismatched knitting needles and glance at the jar of buttons (quite close enough, thank you very much for asking). In a last-ditch effort, I pick up the pink pot-bellied piggy bank and give it a good shake.

The piggy bank rattles and clanks in a rattly, clanky sort of way. Like it's running a little low on pennies. Bailey raises her eyebrow again. Something about the sound is wrong. Too heavy. Too metally. I bite my lip and give the pig another shake.

I peek in the slot on its back.

And instead of coins, there's the gleam of a small, rusted key.

Rachel Bailey smiles.

With shaking fingers, I fumble the stopper from the piggy's tummy, shake the key into my sticky palm and turn to face the wardrobe.

The key slides into the lock. It turns.

The door swings open, and . . .

A Jenga-stack of books tumbles at my feet.

I groan. No bones. No bodies. Just a pile of somebody's old schoolbooks kerflumped across the floor. I'm about to shove the whole pile back in the wardrobe, when the nearest cover catches my eye.

I kneel down, grab the book and hold it up to the moonlight. The handwriting is tightly looped and terribly small, but luckily my reading is better than my spelling (it's a Down syndrome thing).

*Diary of Jane Maypole*

I peer at the rest of the pile. They're all old blue exercise books, like somebody's homework from school, all skinny and dusty, stained with teacup circles and smudged with ink. Some are dog-eared, some still smooth, but written on the front of every single book are the same words: *Diary of Jane Maypole.*

Whizz, bang, fizz. My tummy flips and twirls and fizzes like a firework.

Jane Maypole. Great Aunt Jane.

I've found her missing diaries!

## ★ SEVEN ★

# The Missing Diaries

Before my trembling fingers can open Great Aunt Jane's diaries, the front door opens and closes, footsteps clatter up the stairs and the spare-room door flies open.

I freeze, Great Aunt Jane still clutched in my hands.

Really? Now? Just when I need to be alone?

"Darling!" Auntie G swoops across the room, spotty-greyhound coffee cup in hand, and gathers me (and Great Aunt Jane) into a ginger-biscuit-scented hug. "I'm so sorry I wasn't here to fetch you. Three new pups arrived at the shelter and I couldn't bear them to be lonely. I hope the boys helped you settle in. Where are they?"

She holds me at arm's length and scans the room, like Niko and Oli might be hiding under the bed, or on top of the wardrobe. While her head is turned, I smuggle the diary behind my back and nudge the rest of the pile under the bed with my foot. "Out," I say. "Don't know where Niko went, but Oli's at soccer."

Auntie G's beautiful, smooth forehead crinkles. "Oh, darling. I'm so sorry. I told them to play with you."

My tummy tightens. I don't need "playing with." And why do they need to be told? They used to *want* to hang with me.

Auntie G sighs. "And I meant to make the room lovely for you. But look at it!"

I shrug. "It's OK." The room's a mess. Much worse than when I moved in, actually. Hopefully she won't ask why all the boxes and bags have been upended.

"I'm so sorry, darling. What with Mabel's party this weekend and your mum and dad working and your uncle Lionel never helping with anything to do with Mabel – what on earth they've had against each other all these years, I'll never know, I . . . Gosh!" She stops mid-flow, bends down and picks up a can of Spam. "This stuff must be Great Aunt Jane's. Goes to show how long I've been meaning to tidy up in here. Tell you what . . ." She picks up another can. "Tidying this mess could be our summer project. We might even find her famous diaries!"

"It's really OK," I say quickly. "I just need to hang my dress in the wardrobe."

Auntie G drops her cans and hugs me again. "Of course you do. Look, here's a hanger. Let's pop it on the back of the door for tonight and we'll spruce this place up properly tomorrow. Now," she adds, pulling me into another of her wonderful hugs and kissing the top of my head. "I completely forgot to order Mabel's cake, so if you can make do without any Flower Fairies tonight . . ."

For a moment, my tummy twists. When I was little and used to get homesick, Uncle David was banished to the sofa bed in my room downstairs and Auntie G let me curl up with her and read me the Flower Fairies books. (Along with greyhounds, Flower Fairies are Auntie G's most favorite thing. She actually looks like the Blackberry Fairy, with her dark, dark eyes and frothy black curls.) Even though I'm much too old now, she still reads me one or two before bed when I'm here.

But much as I love Auntie G (and a Flower Fairy or two would be so cozy), right now, more than anything, I need to read Great Aunt Jane's diaries. As absolutely soon as possible. So I nod and we hug again and Auntie G says sorry again. Then she picks her way back around the boxes and bags and closes the door behind her.

As soon as her footsteps fade along the landing, I scoop an armful of books from under the bed, flick on the lamp and fumble to the first page.

Puffs of papery air flap from between the pages and my nose wrinkles. The handwriting is really tricky and I have to skip parts, but I peer and squint and screw up my face and, gradually, the words begin to make sense. I settle tummy-down on the scratchy bedspread and read.

Apparently, when she was little, Miss Batt used to guzzle the top of the milk from the bottles on the Belfrys' doorstep then fill them up with water, so no one was any the wiser. Except, that is, Great Aunt Jane.

When he was young, Mr. Belfry used to pay his friends to mow the churchyard for him. Even when his dad told him not to. And again no one noticed the coins changing hands, except Great Aunt Jane.

And Mr. Belfry's dad was often seen creeping down to the crypt with someone Great Aunt Jane delicately doesn't name, but who very definitely wasn't Mr. Belfry's mum.

For the first time since arriving at St. Jude's Junction, I smile. Great Aunt Jane had a knack for observing details no one else noticed and writing them all down. She wasn't an interfering sticky-beak. She was a brilliant surveiller, just like Grandma Mabel said she was.

In fact, she would have made a marvelous detective. And – my tummy fizzes big time at this thought – everybody says that I'm just like her.

Which means I can be a marvelous detective too.

Only – the fizz in my tummy splutters and dies – detectives need a mystery to solve, don't they? Not just slurped milk or swapped swimsuits. A proper, serious case. And where will I find one of those in St. Jude's Junction?

I flop back against the pillows and stare at the ceiling.

I try thinking like Rachel Bailey. I try thinking like Great Aunt Jane. I try not thinking at all. And shiver by shiver, like a delicious handful of ice cubes down the back of my neck, an answer appears.

Great Aunt Jane's diaries are a mystery all of their own.

I sit up and stare at the wardrobe. I mean, why were they locked away? Why was the key hidden? Unless she wrote something no one was supposed to read. Like a different sort of skeleton in the closet. A secret.

What on earth could it be? Heart thumpity-thumping, I grab the next book and fumble through the pages. More local crimes and badly behaved neighbors, but nothing mysterious. I grab the next book and the next, then another and another. Until there's only one diary left.

This one is smoother than the others, like it's barely been used. With trembling fingers, I trace the date on the front. *June 1973*. It must be close to when she died.

I hold my breath and scrabble to the first page.

*1 Church Lane, June 26th 1973*
*Well, everybody came and it was so lovely to have the house full again. Raymond and Rose with little Lionel and David. And Mabel with Johnny, even though the poor chap should probably have stayed tucked up in bed with that awful cough.*

Hmm. It seems to be about some sort of family party. Great Aunt Jane's family. Mine. There's Great Uncle Raymond and Great Aunt Rose. Uncle Lionel and Uncle David. Even Grandma Mabel and Grandpa Johnny. What could possibly be mysterious about that?

*But I never did tell them my terrible news.*

Ah, this is more like it . . .

*Cherry made her steak and kidney pie and Mabel was sick all over the table. I suspect the dear girl is pregnant. Anyway, Cherry cleaned up the dining room and I cleaned up Mabel. Then I gave her my room, so she would be closer to the bathroom, and I sent Johnny downstairs to the sofa with his bottle of cough syrup, so she would not be disturbed. By then it seemed better to keep my news to myself, at least until the morning.*

*So now I am all cozy in the spare room. Except, how strange! I do hope I have not caught Mabel's sickness.*

My eyes flick to the top of the next page. But there's no more writing. My shoulders slump. There has to be more. What was Great Aunt Jane's terrible news?

I reread the first page. Stare at the next empty one. Look back and forth between the two. Then . . . down the seam between the pages are little, jagged rips of paper. Like a page has been torn out.

A missing page?

I lean closer and Rachel Bailey peers over my shoulder. On the blank piece of paper where the missing page should be, are faint rows of dots and grooves.

Great Aunt Jane's pen marks?

Heart thwacking, I shove the book under the lamp. I finger the dips and hollows. But I can't make out the words.

I need a pencil! Then I can shade the lines and grooves, like when we did leaf prints at school. I glance at Grandma

Mabel's Pip-Squeaks. Too thick, too wet. Then I remember the journal Mum gave me. Looped to the side of *MY AMAZING LIFE* . . . is a small silver pencil.

I fumble it free. Bite my lip. Shade the lines and grooves, until letter by letter, the words from the missing page reappear.

*How odd. I suddenly feel most unwell. Indeed, I think I have been poisoned. My tea tastes like ch*

## ★ EIGHT ★

# A Real Proper Mystery

The fizz in my tummy explodes like a galaxy of stars. Great Aunt Jane was poisoned! In this very room! In this very bed!

Then the killer ripped out her final words and locked every single diary in the wardrobe.

I flop back against my pillow. This is just the mystery I've been waiting for.

A real, proper murder.

Which needs a real, proper detective.

Mizzy the Marvelous smiles at Rachel Bailey. *Just wait till we tell the boys.*

\* \* \*

As soon as I wake up the next morning, I plonk myself cross-legged on the landing between Niko and Oli's bedroom doors.

Uncle David sings in the shower.

The kettle hums then whistles in the kitchen and the sweet, spicy scent of Auntie G's coffee wafts up the stairs. Then the front door opens and closes and her footsteps hurry away down the path.

A bit later, the singing and the shower stop. The bathroom door opens and closes and Uncle David heads back to his bedroom. He pauses in the doorway and glances over his shoulder, one eyebrow raised in my direction, but I pretend to be suddenly fascinated by a feathery swirl in the carpet.

It's a long, cramped wait, but Niko and Oli finally emerge. Before either of them so much as blinks, I leap to my feet and beckon them along the landing to the spare room.

Finger to my lips, I usher them inside and close the door.

"What's with the official secrets act, Miz?" Oli strides over the jumble of bags and boxes and sprawls on the bed. It looks like he slept in his soccer uniform. He rubs his eyes and yawns.

Niko leans against the door and pulls out his phone. He's wearing the same hoodie and jeans as yesterday, but this morning, his fingernails are the exact same shade of pink as his hair. It's a great look and I might need to borrow it, but right now there are more important matters to attend to.

I join Oli on the bed and pat the pile of Great Aunt Jane's notebooks. "These."

"Your homework?" Oli grins and glances at Niko.

Niko doesn't look up from his phone.

I smile. Mizzy the Marvelous has a great sense of humor. "They're Great Aunt Jane's diaries."

Oli looks down at the books. His eyes widen. "For real? Where on earth did you find them?"

I nod at the wardrobe. "In there. Locked up."

Oli's eyes narrow at the wardrobe. Then he looks back at the pile of books. "Locked?"

I nod. This is going better than I dared to hope.

Niko glances up from his phone. "Why would anyone lock Great Aunt Jane's diaries in the wardrobe, Miz?"

This is my moment. Chest puffed up with pride, my words jumble out in a rush. "Somebody poisoned her. Look!"

I shove Great Aunt Jane's torn-out-but-found-again-by-Mizzy-the-Marvelous message under Oli's nose. My chest puffs and puffs. "The page was torn out, but Great Aunt Jane pressed really hard when she wrote, just like I do, and I shaded the words. Like a leaf print."

Oli's eyes are as wide as soccer balls. "Niko, Mizzy says Great Aunt Jane thinks she was poisoned."

I hold my breath as Niko slides his phone in his pocket.

"It's the last note she wrote," I add helpfully. "She died the very same night. In. This. Bed."

Well, I think she did. I still need to verify that bit of information, but Uncle David or Auntie G should be able to help.

Oli turns wonderfully pale and slides down the bedspread to the floor. Niko frowns. I hold my breath and try to look just the right amount of pleased with myself. This is the part where they both tell me how brilliant I am, that I simply have to be Sherlock and they'll be Watsons and together we'll spend the whole, entire summer working out who killed Great Aunt Jane.

Except it isn't.

The corners of Niko's mouth curl. "Nice try, Miz." Still smirking, he picks his way back across the room and out the door. His feet pound down the stairs.

I turn to Oli. So what if Niko doesn't believe me? Oli will. "We can investigate together and work out who killed her. You can be Sherlock. Are you in?" I'm babbling, I know I am, but Oli will want to help. Please let him want to help. He's never turned down a mystery in his life.

Oli glances at Great Aunt Jane's diary on the bed. He glances at the door. Then he leaps to his feet and races after Niko. "Sorry, Miz. Niko's promised he'll play soccer with me. Maybe some Clue tonight," he calls back over his shoulder. "If we're not back too late."

## NINE

# On My Own

My throat aches. Neither of the boys even looked at the diary. They think it's just a game. That I made it all up.

Of course they do. Making stuff up is what I do best. Along with crashing to conclusions and grabbing sticks at the wrong end. But not this time. My tummy knows that Great Aunt Jane's last words are true. She didn't die peacefully in her sleep, like everyone thinks she did. She was murdered.

Every bit of me longs to run after the boys and convince them I'm right, but as I scrabble to the door and grab the handle, something strange and new and solid glues my feet in place.

My fingers slither off the doorknob.

My forehead drops against the door.

Niko and Oli thump down the stairs. There's crashing and banging in the kitchen. A ball bounces in the hall. Then the front door slams and feet pound down the path to the street.

Silence.

Other than Uncle David, who everybody knows doesn't count, I'm all alone again.

But a small voice mumbles at the back of my brain. It might be Rachel Bailey. It might even be Great Aunt Jane. *What if this is how it's supposed to be?*

After all, I found Great Aunt Jane's diaries. I spotted the ripped-out page. I shaded her grooved last words. I didn't need anybody's help. Which means – I swallow hard – I can solve her murder on my own.

My heart starts to thwump. This time, I'll do it properly. No more crashing to conclusions. No more getting things wrong. I'll write proper case notes, like Great Aunt Jane did in her diaries. I'll make a list of suspects, and I'll interview them and write down all their answers. Then I'll put the clues together and solve the case. And on the weekend, when I've solved the mystery all on my own, I'll put on my Rachel-Bailey dress and I'll get some makeup from somewhere and I'll unmask the murderer at Grandma Mabel's party, in front of Mum and Dad and Niko and Oli and my whole, entire family.

Then we'll see who thinks I'm a baby.

I grab my *MY AMAZING LIFE* journal. There, beside it on the bedside table, just waiting to be useful, are Grandma Mabel's Pip-Squeaks. Perfect. I won't just have case notes. I'll have *color-coded* case notes. I sit cross-legged on the scratchy bedspread and at the top of the first page, in *dinky pink* (my most favorite color), I print:

MIZZY THE MAHVELLUS CAS NOTS

Underneath, I list everything Great Aunt Jane wrote about her last evening.

- FAMILY PARTY
- TERRERBUL NUZ
- GRAMPA JONNEE COFF
- GRANMA MABEL SICK
- POYZUN
- TEE TAYSTED LIKE CH— SUMTHING??

I chew the end of my Pip-Squeak. What was Great Aunt Jane's terrible news? What was in her tea that tasted like ch-something? And who put it there?

Most important of all, who tore out her last words about poison and locked her diaries in the wardrobe?

I scribble down my questions, just like Rachel Bailey. Then I draw my family tree. Everyone who was at Great Aunt Jane's party on the night she died.

- GRATE UNKEL RAYMUND
- GRATE ANT ROZE
- UNKEL LIYONELL
- UNKEL DAYVID
- GRANMA MABEL
- GRAMPA JONNEE

And of course, Cherry-someone-or-other, who made the steak and kidney pie. I add her name with a question mark beside it.

- CHERREE SUMBODEE ?

I sit back on my heels and admire my work.

# MY FAMILY TREE

NEFFUE —— GRATE ANT JANE
**VICTIM**

 +

GRATE ANT ROZE
SUSSPEKT

GRATE UNKEL RAYMUND
SUSSPEKT

 +

ANTY G  UNKEL DAYVID  UNKEL LIYONELL
(NOT BAWN YET)  SUSSPEKT  SUSSPEKT

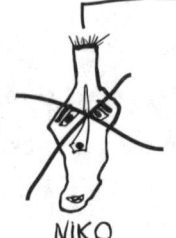  

NIKO  OLI
(NOT BAWN YET) (NOT BAWN YET)

CHERREE SUMBODEE?
(NOT FAMILY)

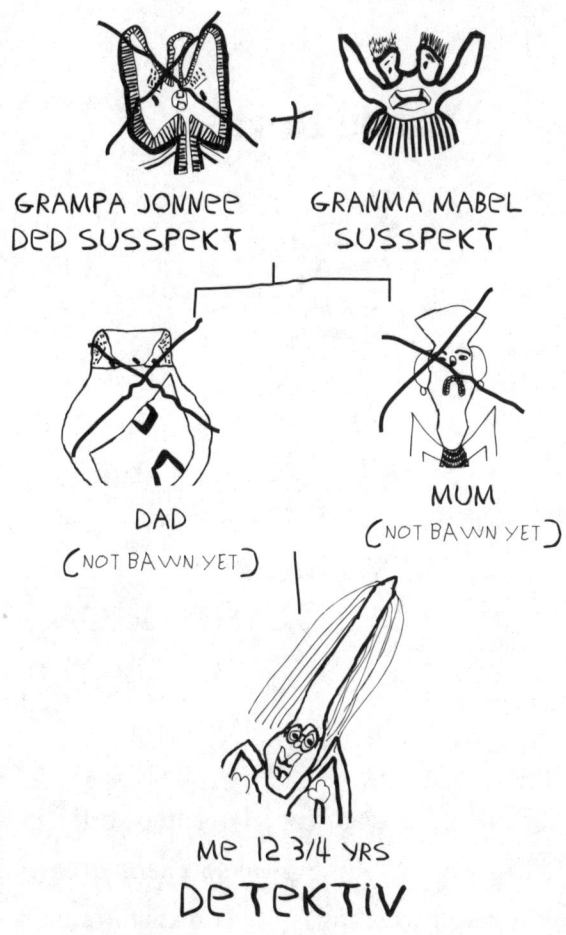

Too bad Grandpa Johnny is dead and I haven't a clue who this Cherry person is, but everyone else is alive and waiting to be interviewed by yours truly.

Rachel Bailey nods her approval and I smile back at her.

Mizzy the Marvelous is ready to investigate.

# Uncle David

SUSSPEKT: UNKEL DAYVID
RELAYSHUNSHIP TO GRATE ANT JANE:
GRATE NEFFUE
AGE ON JOON 26TH 1973: 10

It takes me all morning, but finally I have a list of very clever questions. I close my notebook and stuff it under my pillow (along with my Pip-Squeaks). Then, tummy fizzing and flipping and whirling, I race downstairs to interview my first suspect.

Uncle David is Dad's cousin. Great Aunt Rose and Great Uncle Raymond are his mum and dad and he's their second son. Uncle Lionel is his brother, which is weird because they don't look a thing alike.

Actually, he's not a very likely suspect, seeing as he was only ten when Great Aunt Jane died. But he was at her party and he's right here, right now, so he seems like a good place to start. And he's a numbers person, so he'll likely remember the exact date Great Aunt Jane died.

I hurry through the kitchen to Uncle David's office, throw open the door and march inside.

Uncle David is hunched over his computer and doesn't seem to notice me.

I go out and come back in.

Uncle David doesn't flicker.

I cough.

Uncle David doesn't flinch.

This is not what I planned. Pretending my legs are as long as Rachel Bailey's, I stride up to his desk, drape an arm across the back of his chair and whisper, "Uncle David?" in his ear.

"Hmmm?"

His eyes stay glued to the screen. Rows and rows of numbers, arranged in columns. Train times probably.

Uncle David is responsible for timetabling all the trains this side of London.

I pull out my notebook and a boring *pussy willow gray* Pip-Squeak. "When did Great Aunt Jane die?" I ask as casually as possible.

Uncle David's eyes stay fixed on the computer and his fingers keep typing. "Not right now, Miz."

I roll my eyes behind his back. Helpfulness is not Uncle David's strong point. "When would be convenient?" I ask.

"Hmmm?"

"When can I talk to you?" I shout a bit, like people do for me when they think I don't understand.

Uncle David sighs and stops typing. "Why do you want to know about Great Aunt Jane?"

My mind goes blank. I'm meant to be asking questions, not answering them. "Oh, just homework," I manage at last. "A family tree. Who was born when and died when and . . . um . . . how they died?" Not bad. Rachel Bailey nods her approval.

One of Uncle David's eyebrows shoots toward his (very hairless) hairline and the apple thing above his collar bulges. His eyes stay fixed on his computer screen. "June 26th, 1973. In her sleep."

Perfect. An exact match for her last diary entry. I scribble down the date. "Anything else?" I prompt. "Anything about the night before she died?"

Uncle David leans closer to his screen. Columns of numbers zoom up and down as he scrolls. "There was a party. Here."

I nod. "And?"

His apple thingy bobs again and his bottom jaw jerks. Like when you karate chop yourself below the knee and your foot flies up in the air. "We ate steak and kidney pie for dinner, looked at stamps and went to bed. And in the morning, she was dead."

"You must remember more than that," I blurt. "Anything strange? Anything odd –"

It's like I've pulled a plug. Uncle David stiffens. "Time's up, Mizzy," he says. "Scat."

# Rumbled

So, Great Aunt Jane died on the very night she thought she was being poisoned. June 26th, 1973. And there was a party. And everyone ate steak and kidney pie.

But other than confirming what I already know, my first interview was a disaster.

More Mr. Bean than Rachel Bailey.

Even Sherlock and Two Watsons would have been embarrassed.

I close Uncle David's door behind me and I'm about to scurry back up to the spare room and lock myself in the wardrobe until my face stops burning. But, as I scrabble through the kitchen, Oli looks up from his spot on the table.

I freeze mid-scrabble. He's digging at his soccer cleats with a spoon and, by the number of little dried-mud hexagons scattered around him, he must have been home for a while.

My face burns a hundred degrees hotter. I was so busy with Uncle David, I didn't even hear him come in. But *he* must have heard at least some of my so-called interview.

His eyes narrow. "What are you up to, Miz?"

I take a steadying breath and join him at the table – all willowy and casual-like. "Nothing. Just chatting with your dad."

Auntie G has left the Shreddies out and a sticky note with pink felt-pen fairy wings telling us to help ourselves. I flick dried mud from my bowl and pour the cereal in, pretending to be fascinated by each Shreddie.

"Dad doesn't chat," says Oli.

I nibble a Shreddie. "He chats to me."

Oli snorts. "That wasn't chatting. He was mad. I heard him. And Dad doesn't lose his cool easily."

Interesting. So, Oli noticed Uncle David was rattled too. I focus on my Shreddies, picking out the dry ones with long, elegant fingers and eating them one at a time (Mizzy the Marvelous can take or leave food).

Oli stabs at his boot with the butter knife and yanks out a particularly large honeycomb of mud from between the cleats. "You're such a fibber, Miz. What was all that about Great Aunt What's-her-face?"

My tummy flutters. I wonder . . . can I tell Oli the truth? Can we play Sherlock and One Watson, only this time, I'll be Sherlock and it'll be for real?

But then I sigh. Games belong with the old Oli. This new one, with the deep voice and the cheekbones and the size twenty-three feet – I barely recognize him, let alone trust him. I showed him Great Aunt Jane's diaries and he didn't even care.

I pick at another Shreddie and launch into my brilliant new cover story about the family-tree-summer-holiday project for school. When I'm finished, Oli's eyes narrow again. I open mine as wide as possible and stare back at him.

But Oli, it seems, knows me too well. "A family tree?" he says.

I nod.

"For school?" he says.

"Yup."

"And you're going to interview all the oldies?"

"Uh-huh."

"Right, Miz. And I'm the King of England."

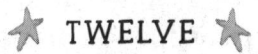

## TWELVE

# Great Aunt Rose

SUSSPEKT: GRATE ANT ROZE
RELAYSHUNSHIP TO GRATE ANT JANE:
NEECE (BY MARRIDGE)
AGE ON JOON 26TH 1973: 30ISH

After jotting down Uncle David's (very short) answers about steak and kidney pie and Great Aunt Jane being dead in the morning, I set off for his parents' house.

Great Aunt Rose and Great Uncle Raymond's house. The new estate they live on is only two streets away from Auntie G's, which means I can walk there. This makes them next on my list.

Hopefully, this interview will go better than the first one. Other than Uncle David confirming when Great Aunt

Jane died, it was a teensy bit of a disaster. Not to mention Oli's already worked out I'm up to something. I'll have to be a lot more marvelous and a lot more careful this time.

The sun warms my shoulders and the air smells of mown grass and all kinds of flowers. Miss Batt's lace curtains twitch and Mr. Belfry freezes, rake in hand, to watch me pass, but I ignore them both and focus on my new Rachel-Bailey walk. Leggy and purposeful, but slow enough to think about what all the different Pip-Squeaks colors can mean in my investigation.

I'm just choosing the perfect shades for Great Uncle Raymond and Great Aunt Rose, when there's a sudden rush of footsteps on the pavement and Oli falls into step beside me.

"Where are you off to?" he says.

Uh-oh. My brain is stuck on *Brussel sproutlet*. Luckily Rachel Bailey comes to the rescue. "Out."

Oli frowns. "What kind of out?"

Bailey's got it covered. "The outside kind."

"Seriously, Miz, are you sure you should be out on your own?"

My tummy tightens. I bet he's worried I'll get lost and he'll be blamed. "Quite sure, thank you," I say.

"Maybe I'll just tag along."

"I'm fine."

"Yeah, right. What about the time you got on the bus in Putney and ended up in Brighton or Bournemouth or –"

"That was last year," I interrupt. "And I'm not on a bus, am I?"

Oli's cheekbones turn pink. He runs a hand through his bangs and looks away. But he doesn't leave my side. "Well, Mum made me promise to keep an eye on you, so I'm coming along, like it or not."

I *don't* like it. Oli doesn't want to be my Watson anymore, and if he finds out what I'm doing he'll just call me babyish again. Most of all, this is *my* investigation and Mizzy the Marvelous needs to solve it on her own.

But I don't want Oli more suspicious of my movements than he already is. I'll just have to make sure my next interviews seem completely family-tree-ish, so he doesn't figure out what I'm up to.

I shrug. "It's a free country."

We walk in silence. Well, Oli whistles, but I'm focused on my next suspect.

Great Uncle Raymond is Grandma Mabel's brother. I think he's younger than her, not that he behaves like it. He's so bossy and grand, it's easy to think he's the oldest in the family. Plus, he looks like he's practically dead. He's not a swimmer, like Grandma Mabel. He just sits in his fancy leather chair and writes long, boring novels about people from long ago. And when he's not writing his boring books, he drones on about them at long, boring length.

Luckily for me (because I can interview two suspects in the same place), Great Uncle Raymond is married to Great Aunt Rose, who makes up for him by being almost as lovely as Auntie G. Mum says she's very "artistic." She's a painter, but I don't think that's quite what Mum means.

Anyway, I haven't been to Great Uncle Raymond's house since I was seven. Apparently, he thinks it's much easier for everyone if we always meet at Auntie G's. But this is the real story. The last time I visited, I knocked over one of Great Uncle Raymond's prized lamps. One of those really expensive ones, with all the bits of colored glass. And I left sticky handprints on his ever-so-tasteful wallpaper. You'd have thought I'd killed somebody, the fuss he made. Even now, my face sizzles at the memory.

Gossington Avenue is the poshest street in St. Jude's Junction. All the houses are big and fancy, hidden from the road by big, fancy hedges. If any murderers live here, they're probably big and fancy too. Which could, in fact, be the point. Maybe Raymond poisoned Great Aunt Jane for her money. He did get her house when she died, didn't he? I study the houses carefully as we pass, peering through each gate at the front doors, in case I spot a murderous sort of color. Or an axe on the doorstep.

Oli, it seems, has guessed where I'm heading. "Here we are," he says, as we reach number sixty-seven. He opens the gate and heads up the drive to the front door (blood red, but I mustn't crash to conclusions). "My grandparents do know you're coming, Miz, don't they? They might want to lock up the lamps."

"Of course they know I'm coming." I push past Oli and knock on the colossal door.

Actually, they don't know I'm coming. I wasn't going to give my suspects a chance to say no, or time to prepare for my questions. It didn't cross my mind they might be out.

Luckily, Great Aunt Rose opens the door.

"Mizzy! And . . . Oli?" She stoops to kiss my cheek with her wrinkled lips, tiptoes to peck Oli's. "My favorite great niece and grandson! Darlings! How delightful!"

She's wearing her usual black leggings and sweater. But unlike when we see her at Auntie G's – when she's always impossibly sleek and elegant for an almost-eighty-five-year-old – every bit of her is smeared with paint. Her sweater, her leggings, her bare feet and hands and face are all splashed with as many different colors as my Pip-Squeaks. The tip of her nose is pea green.

I'm gaping at all her colors like a goldfish. Oli glances at my open mouth, then turns back to Great Aunt Rose. "We've come about Mizzy's project?"

I jump. Is Oli coming to my rescue, or dropping me in into trouble? "The family tree I'm doing for school," I add. "It's my summer project and Great Uncle Raymond promised he'd help."

I hold my breath. Hopefully, Great Aunt Rose will just think he's forgotten to tell her.

Her forehead creases briefly – lavender and lime mixing with a blob of tangerine. Then she smiles and nods. "Of course, darlings, of course. Step right in."

Oli throws me a glance I can't read – part suspicious, part admiring. I give him my best Rachel-Bailey nod, like everything is going exactly to plan. If I can just convince Great Uncle Raymond I arranged our visit with Great Aunt Rose, then none of them will be any the wiser.

I take a deep, steadying breath and follow Great Aunt Rose into the house, Oli trailing along behind. The hall smells like lemons and I'm tempted to press creased-palm handprints onto the pale yellow wallpaper. But I don't. Not yet, anyway.

"Raymond's writing in his cave," Great Aunt Rose whispers, tiptoeing to a halt beside a firmly closed door. She holds a finger to her lips. From behind the door, there's a faint sound of typing. Great Uncle Raymond must be sitting in his leather chair, in his purple velvet jacket, clicking away on his typewriter.

I can't wait to sink my teeth into him. But Great Aunt Rose says, "He doesn't usually stop for tea until eleven and he hates to be disturbed. Maybe I can help you, in the meantime. Come on through to the studio."

Great Aunt Rose's studio is at the far end of their massive garden. It's one large room, with massive churchy windows and an indoor-balcony thing around half of the towering ceiling. It stinks of paint, and what looks like a giant bedsheet is spread across the floor.

Great Aunt Rose creaks to her knees in front of the bedsheet. One corner is smeared with an exploded rainbow, but the rest is empty and white. She arranges five or six pots of paint on the floor beside the sheet, then brushes and dabs and smears more colors all over another corner. "I just need to finish this part," she says. "Have a look around and I'll give you a shout when I'm ready."

I'd rather get started on the interview, but my Uncle David disaster has taught me a bit about patience. Leaving Great Aunt Rose on her hands and knees with her rainbow, I drag Oli around the studio.

We study pots of paint and jam jars crammed with paintbrushes. We peer through the window and study a robin in the rose bushes. We gaze up at the indoor-balcony thing above our heads. Flashes of colorful canvases peek through the railings and when it's obvious Great Aunt Rose isn't going to be ready for us anytime soon, I lead Oli up the spiral metal staircase.

We're met by row after row of portraits, stacked side by side on the balcony floor. I'm used to seeing Great Aunt Rose's paintings of flowers and rainbows and stuff like that. But these are people. Small boys, to be precise. Three of them, painted at all different ages.

Oli points at a serious boy of about nine or ten, with screwed-up brown eyes. "There's Dad! I'd know that frown anywhere."

He's right. It's easy to pick out Uncle David. I point at another painting. "And that's Uncle Lionel." Even in the portraits of them as kids, they don't look at all alike.

Oli joins me in front of a skinny kid with blond curls and blue eyes. "Definitely Lionel," he agrees. Then he pauses and shakes his head. "Actually, I think it's your dad."

"Lionel," I say.

"Your dad. Isn't it?" Oli tips the canvas forward and peers at a handwritten scrawl on the back. "Yup. It says Stephen."

He's right. It *is* Dad. How strange. Dad and Uncle Lionel are cousins, of course, but they don't look much alike these days. But here, as kids, they could be twins.

I scan the balcony, trying to pick out more Dads and Lionels, until Great Aunt Rose's voice rises anxiously up the stairs, behind us. "Not up there, darlings. Do come down."

Great Aunt Rose has started up the spiral staircase to fetch us. The tip of her nose is orange and pink now, as well as pea green, and the whites of her eyes are huge. "Whatever were you doing up there?" There's a shake in her voice that wasn't there before.

"You said to look around," I answer, with my most innocent I'm-not-a-detective lisp.

"Yes, but not up there. Those paintings aren't for looking at."

The paintings aren't for looking at? "But isn't that the point of paintings?" I say.

"Not those ones." Great Aunt Rose grabs my hand and marches me back downstairs to the bedsheet. "Now," she asks, her voice strangely squeaky. "What was it you wanted to ask me?"

I really want to ask her about the paintings of Dad and Uncle Lionel and why we're not supposed to look at them, but I don't want to shut her up, like I did with Uncle David. So, I turn my back firmly on the staircase and, Rachel-Bailey-casual-as-possible, say, "Oh, dates and stuff. When people were born and . . . um . . . when they died."

Great Aunt Rose gives a funny little laugh. "Oh, that's easy. Raymond was born in 1939 and I was born in 1940."

I pull out my notebook and jot this down.

*Grasshopper green* for Great Aunt Rose, *sapling beige* for Great Uncle Raymond. "And the boys?" I ask. "Uncle Lionel and Uncle David?"

"Hmmm?" Great Aunt Rose kneels down and fiddles with a paint pot. Unscrews the lid then tightens it again. Three times.

I try again. "When was your eldest son, Lionel, born?"

"Lionel, you say?" Great Aunt Jane fiddles with another pot. "1962," she says at last.

I use *jelly-bean blue* for Uncle Lionel, an almost perfect match for his eyes. "And David?"

"Hmmm . . . let me see . . ." Great Aunt Rose fiddles with each of her pots in turn.

Oli answers for her. "1963."

I note that down too, in Uncle David's *pussy willow gray*. When I look up, Great Aunt Rose's eyes are even wider than before and her face has turned beetroot red. She frowns at my notebook. Then she frowns at me. "I've just remembered . . . Raymond's out and I have an appointment . . . with . . . with . . . Must rush."

And, without another word, Great Aunt Rose scrabbles to her feet, scuttles straight across her newly painted bedsheet and disappears through the studio door.

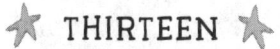# THIRTEEN

# Great Uncle Raymond

SUSSPEKT: GRATE UNKEL RAYMUND
RELAYSHUNSHIP TO GRATE ANT JANE:
NEFFUE
AGE ON JOON 26TH 1973: 34

Great Aunt Rose hurries down Gossington Avenue in her bare feet, toes, clothes and hair all splattered with paint.

Oli stares after her and taps the side of his head. "Cuckoo."

I nod, but I'm wondering . . . might Great Aunt Rose in fact be more *guilty* than *cuckoo*? Why didn't she want us going upstairs in the studio? Why are the paintings of Dad and Uncle Lionel and Uncle David not for looking at? Why did she just run away? I hadn't even mentioned Great Aunt Jane.

At the corner of the street, Great Aunt Rose glances back at us over her shoulder. I grab Oli's arm and start walking in the other direction. When Great Aunt Rose is safely out of sight, I march back up to the blood-red door.

Oli joins me on the doorstep. "Mizzy, she said he was out . . ."

A likely story. He was typing, wasn't he? I duck around the side of the house, through the gate and in through the kitchen door, Oli trailing behind me. As we reach the hallway, I hold my finger to my lips, just like Great Aunt Rose did, and point to Great Uncle Raymond's "cave."

In the empty house, the typewriter keys click like gunshots.

I take a deep breath, then throw open the door and barge inside.

The "cave" actually couldn't be less cave-like. There's a wall of windows on one side and the sun streams across Great Uncle Raymond's bookshelves.

Perfect lighting to watch him hit the ceiling.

As he lands back in his white leather chair, one hand grabs the lamp beside him. "Mizzy!" he says, his other hand smoothing his sweep of silver hair. "And . . . Niko? I mean, Oli? What a surprise! Rose never mentioned you were coming."

"Didn't she?" I say, smooth as Rachel Bailey. "I do hope we're not interrupting you."

"No, no . . . not at all," Great Uncle Raymond answers, looking very much interrupted. His face has a purple tinge, like his velvet jacket. "Have a seat. Over there on the sofa," he adds quickly, pointing to a particularly lampless part of the room.

I join Oli on the pale cream sofa and sink into the softest cushions ever. It's like sitting in a bowl of whipped cream. Actually, the whole room is cream. Pale cream, or dark cream, or frothy-whipped-creamish white. Even a marshmallow would leave marks, let alone a girl with a natural talent for being sticky.

There's the wall of windows and two of the other walls are broken up with Great Aunt Rose's paintings. Not like the colorful stuff in the studio – all the paintings here are creamy flowers and snowy landscapes, square and bulgy but very tasteful. The last wall has a built-in bookcase (white) and – the only splash of color in the whole place (other than Great Uncle Raymond's purple jacket) – a patchwork of different-color books.

This isn't the room of someone with something to hide. But maybe that's the point.

Great Uncle Raymond leans back in his chair and

smooths a blanket over his lap (cream squares, with white criss-crossed lines), taking his time, like he's ironing. No fear, or nervousness, or guilt – just a fussy old bird arranging his nest. He seemed sprightly enough when he hit the ceiling just now, but up close he's like one of those fossils at the Natural History Museum.

Could such an ancient person actually murder anyone?

But of course, Great Aunt Jane was poisoned over fifty years ago. Great Uncle Raymond would have been younger than Mum and Dad are now.

"Rose is in the studio," he says, wheezing a little. "Can't disturb the old girl while she's creating. Now, to what do I owe this great honor?"

"I'm doing a summer project for school," I explain. "A family tree."

Oli snorts, but Great Uncle Raymond's face gets even wrinklier as he smiles. "Ah, a school project. I expect you want my advice on writing styles. Or is it famous relatives you're after?"

Neither. "Both." Ooh, I'm good at this. Mizzy the Marvelous-Sucker-Upperer.

Great Uncle Raymond's smile widens. "Grand plan, young Mizzy. Now, you'll be wanting a list of my works, I imagine."

It's a long list, but eventually Great Uncle Raymond reaches the end. Oli's head lolls back on the sofa and a line of dribble runs down his chin.

"Is there anything else I can help you with, dear?" Great Uncle Raymond asks.

I fight the urge to yawn. "Yes, please. I need to know about the rest of the family too."

"How silly of me! Of course you do." Great Uncle Raymond smiles, like he never feels silly about anything. "Now, you know Rose is a very-much-admired artist?"

I know she's a paint-smeared cuckoo, with a memory problem when it comes to the birth of her own children. But I nod politely and try to look like her admiredness is all I ever think about.

"Perhaps you could include some photographs of her better-known works?" He waves his hand again, taking in a sweep of creamy-white flowers and snowscapes.

"They're lovely," I say. "But it's meant to be people who are related to me. DNA-related. Like your children and sisters and parents. And . . . um . . . aunts."

"Ah yes, of course. Well, not much I can tell you about David and Lionel. Born so close together, people always thought they were twins. Though they're as different as myself and my sister, Mabel." Great Uncle Raymond tugs at the silk scarf thing around his neck and clears his throat. "David was always into trains and Lionel – apart from his plants – was a people-person. Thought he might make a writer for a while – great insight into what makes people tick – but he got caught up with helping his orphans."

Oli gives a little snore and curls his legs up onto the sofa. I scribble in my book in *sapling beige*.

- BOYZ LIK TWINZ
- DAYVID TRAYNZ
- LIYONELL PLANTZ AND ORFANZ

Great Uncle Raymond smooths an invisible crease on the sleeve of his velvet jacket. "My father was an only child, but Mummy had two sisters. Aunt Sarah and Aunt Jane – my favorite. And last but not least, there's Mabel. My sister and your grandmother, of course. I'm sure you know quite enough about her already."

I nod. Grandma Mabel is far too dotty and sweet to be a suspect. "Quite enough, thanks. But I don't know much about Great Aunt Jane. Other than she was a very good noticer."

Great Uncle Raymond throws back his head and laughs so hard, I'm scared for his skinny old neck. Oli sits bolt upright, eyes soccer ball wide.

"That's one word for it!" Great Uncle Raymond laughs again, then coughs in an about-to-croak sort of way. At last he catches his breath. "Dear Aunt Jane. She was such a busybody. Always poking her nose into other people's business and getting the wrong end of the stick. Couldn't help but love the old girl though. An absolute gem."

"How'd she die?" I ask, aiming for I'm-barely-even-interested.

Great Uncle Raymond doesn't miss a beat. "In her sleep."

"Nothing strange?"

He shrugs. "Oh, my dear girl. It was such a long time ago. She invited us down for dinner. Said she had some important news to tell us. But her housekeeper – Cherry Baker, or Butcher, I think it was – made steak and kidney pie and by the time we'd ploughed through it, Jane had forgotten all about her news, poor old duck. By the next morning, she was dead."

Nothing new, but I make notes in my book anyway. Great Uncle Raymond leans forward in his chair and Oli shuffles closer on the sofa, so I take a bit longer than I need to. Eventually, I look up and smile.

Time to shake things up a bit, I think. "And her wardrobe?" I ask.

Great Uncle Raymond suddenly looks very small inside his clothes. "Her wardrobe?"

"The one in the spare room," I add helpfully. "I was wondering if you know what's inside. It's locked."

Great Uncle Raymond makes a sound like a drowning duck at the Ladies' Pond. "Is it? You're quite sure it isn't just old and stuck?"

I nod. Slowly. Taking my time.

Beads of sweat gleam on Great Uncle Raymond's forehead. He pats at them with a huge white hankie, which has suddenly appeared in his hands. "You must be mistaken, dear. We lived in that house for years after Jane died. That is, before we gave it to your parents, Oli," he adds quickly. "The wardrobe in the spare room was never locked. I don't even remember if there was a key. Or any of her funny old diaries or . . . Goodness me, is that the time?"

Great Uncle Raymond clutches the arms of his chair with knobbly hands and creaks (surprisingly quickly) to his feet. "I hate to rush you off like this," he says, "but I've just remembered. My agent will be calling any moment."

And for the second time today, Oli and I are chucked out into the street.

## FOURTEEN

# An Offer of Help

Oli waits until we turn off Gossington Avenue, then he explodes like a dropped can of Coke.

"School project, my bum. You think you're Sherlock Holmes right now, not Watson at all."

Uh-oh. I shrug and keep on walking.

But Oli's legs are much longer than my pretend-Rachel-Bailey ones. He catches me up in no time. "Seriously, Miz, what are you up to? All this about Great Aunt Jane's death – it's what upset Dad too, isn't it? At least he's strong enough to take it. I thought you'd killed my grandad."

So did I. But it was worth it. Lots of lovely new clues. I concentrate on swinging my Rachel-Bailey legs, like I've much more important things on my mind than cousins and what they might, or might not, want to know.

"Come on, Miz," says Oli. "You're up to something, I know it. Why are you suddenly so interested in a dead great great aunt and her wardrobe?"

My steps slow. If only I could tell Oli everything, like in the good old days.

But I did tell him, didn't I? And he didn't believe me. "You really think she was murdered, don't you?" Oli asks.

"Yes —" Oops. That was more Mizzy than Rachel Bailey. I try to look like I was talking about something else. *Yes, I like broccoli . . . how about you?* But my brain is in black-hole mode and Oli is staring at me like I'm actually important again.

Would it really hurt to share my investigation with him? Just a little bit.

I check over my shoulder. A single car crawls around the corner, onto Gossington Avenue. I watch until it's safely out of sight, then lower my voice, so Oli has to bend down to hear me. "I think the person who ripped out her last message is the killer."

Oli stays bent over, like he's waiting for someone to leapfrog him. "Go on."

He isn't smirking. He isn't laughing. "Did you see his face when I asked about the wardrobe?" I say eagerly.

Oli nods. "And you never even mentioned a key, or the diaries."

Exactly. My words tumble over themselves. "I think it means Great Uncle Raymond locked his aunt's diaries in the wardrobe. Which means it was probably him that ripped out the page. Which means he killed her."

I hold my breath. Please don't let him laugh.

A cyclist wobbles past and Oli straightens up to watch. Eventually, the bike disappears round the corner and Oli looks back at me, his eyes wonderfully, gloriously serious. "It's quite a leap, Miz. My grandad ripped out a weirdo message he may or may not have read and he locked up some old diaries in a wardrobe and this means he murdered our great great aunt?"

I nod.

"A leap and an accusation."

I nod again.

"You don't like my grandad, do you?"

"Neither do you," I point out.

Oli laughs. "No, he's a pompous fool. But that doesn't make him a murderer."

"Then why was he so scared when I mentioned the wardrobe?"

Oli stops laughing. "He was scared, wasn't he? My gran got all bothered too, and you hadn't mentioned any kind of furniture. What was that about?"

Exactly. "I don't know. Not yet. But I'm going to find out."

A smile spreads across Oli's face. "Just like old times, eh, Mizzy-Moo?" He drapes an arm around my shoulder. "I can help you, when I'm not training."

I open my mouth, but no sound comes out. There's nothing I'd like more than to team up with Oli again – except this time I'd be Rachel Bailey, and he'd be Watson all on his own, and he'd stop calling me Mizzy-Moo.

But what if he's only offering because Niko put him up to it? Or Auntie G guilted him into "playing" with me? My tummy shrinks into a cold, hard lump. And how can I prove myself to him and Niko, not to mention Mum and Dad and anyone else who thinks I'm a helpless baby, unless I solve the mystery of Great Aunt Jane's murder all on my own?

Like I'm ripping out my own heart, I slide out from under Oli's arm and walk off down the street, as tall as my little legs will let me.

"No, thanks," I call back over my shoulder. "I've got it covered."

# FIFTEEN

# Cherry Baker-or-Butcher

SUSSPEKT: CHERREE BAYKA-OR-BUTCHA
RELAYSHUNSHIP TO GRATE ANT JANE:
HOWSS KEEPA
AGE ON JOON 26TH 1973: 40ISH

For the first time in my life, I really do seem to have things covered. The second round of interviews went so much better than Uncle David's.

After supper, I dodge Oli's meaningful looks, sidestep Auntie G's invitation to read the Flower Fairies and race upstairs to the spare room.

I barely notice the old-lady smell anymore, or the jumble of stuff spread across the floor. This is my room now. Investigation headquarters. I pull my notebook and

Pip-Squeaks out from under my pillow (where I stashed them earlier – just in case) and pore over my case notes.

With Great Aunt Jane's diary entry and my first three interviews, I now know she threw a family party for everyone because she had terrible news to share. Cherry Baker-or-Butcher made steak and kidney pie. Grandma Mabel was sick and Great Aunt Jane put her to bed in her own room. Grandpa Johnny had a terrible cough. Great Aunt Jane decided to save her news for the morning and went to bed in the spare room. She thought somebody had poisoned her, because her tea tasted like something beginning with 'ch,' and the next morning she was dead.

Then somebody ripped the page out of her diary where she wrote about being poisoned and locked her diaries in the wardrobe.

I chew the end of a Pip-Squeak and stare at my new clues. Great Aunt Rose has paintings upstairs in her studio that no one is supposed to look at and Dad and Uncle Lionel used to look like twins. Great Uncle Raymond knew about the wardrobe being locked and about the key and he seemed to know about Great Aunt Jane's diaries being locked up inside. And he got terribly flustered about it all.

I munch the Pip-Squeak a bit more. I'm not sure what Great Aunt Rose's paintings mean, but if my sticks aren't upside down and back to front, the Great Uncle Raymond clues make him a prime suspect for both the ripping out of the missing page and the poisoning.

Rachel Bailey nods and my chest puffs.

But I mustn't get ahead of myself, must I? No more crashing to conclusions. I need to interview everybody. And next on my list is what's-her-name. Cherry Baker-or-Butcher, Great Uncle Raymond called her.

Now I have a last name for her, I should be able to find out if she's still alive and, if so, where she lives (fingers crossed within walking distance of Auntie G's).

One of the perks of having no sense of direction is that Mum and Dad caved and got me a phone. It's meant for tracking me if I'm out of sight for more than ten seconds, but that's not what I use it for now. I get to work on Google.

There are three Cherry Bakers – a writer, a singer and a lady who's very keen to help you keep your back safe. I don't think she means from stabbing, so I keep searching. Anyway, Great Aunt Jane's Cherry would be well into her eighties by now, and these three look much younger.

But there's only one Cherry Butcher. I click on the link and peer at the screen.

My tummy fizzes immediately. It's a recent article from the local paper about a care home in the next village over from St. Jude's Junction, Such Pelham. Something to do with a new activity program involving a tambourine, a beach ball and a parrot. There's even a very small, blurry picture of a rather cross-looking old lady.

I laugh out loud. This must be her. Right sort of age, right sort of location.

Perfect.

Only it isn't, is it? My heart sinks. Such Pelham is the perfectly *wrong* sort of location. Such Pelham is over five miles from St. Jude's Junction.

How on earth will I get there on my own?

I spend the next morning eating Shreddies at the kitchen counter and studying bus timetables on my phone. But they might as well be written in those Egyptian picture thingies.

I glance at Uncle David's door. Would he drive me? Very-likely-probably not. Since my attempt to interview him, he's paying me even less attention than usual.

I'm just wondering if I can tackle the five or so miles to Such Pelham on foot – and whether breadcrumbs or bits of wool make a better trail to guide me back home again – when the back door opens and (spotty-greyhound cup in hand) Auntie G appears in the kitchen.

She joins me at the counter and starts rifling through the drawers. "Where's that shopping list . . ." she mutters, then turns and studies the patchwork of postcards and sticky notes on the fridge. "Ah! There it is. Right. Miz, I need to pop out. David thinks Mabel's birthday balloons should match the different tube lines and there's a shop in Such Pelham that has all sorts of colors."

She doesn't notice me jump. "Can I come?" I ask, in my best I-really-really-want-to-but-I-couldn't-care-less-if-you-say-no voice. "I need to work on my family tree. At the library."


Auntie G drops me at the library (she's just like Mum when it comes to reading and writing). She's ever so sorry, but she can only leave me there for an hour. Let's hope it's enough time.

I bend down to tug at my socks and by the time I've straightened up, Auntie G's battered old Mini is out of sight. I wait a moment, just to make sure she hasn't forgotten anything, then pull out my phone and hurry along the main street in what I hope is the right direction for Dunwerkin Care Home.

After twenty minutes (and a trip along the main street the other way), I finally reach my destination. I wait another five minutes on the doorstep for someone to let me in. Then another two, while a woman with purple hair searches for a pen to sign me into the visitors' book. As Cherry Butcher's granddaughter.

By the time I'm shown through to a small, dark sitting room, there's only fifteen minutes left for my interview.

The sitting room is stuffed with assorted old people, a carer in a pink uniform who doesn't look much older than me and a lime-green parrot. There's a tang of overcooked sprouts – which is weird, because it's just after breakfast – and most of the biddies are asleep, slumped in their stiff-backed armchairs, mouths open.

Only one old lady is awake. She's shaking a tambourine, while the parrot nudges a beach ball around the room with its beak. When I enter, she stops shaking the tambourine, screws up her eyes and glares. Just like the blurry photo in the newspaper article.

The parrot keeps pushing the beach ball, but the carer turns and follows Cherry's gaze. "Yes?" she asks with a bored sigh.

I repeat my part about being Cherry's granddaughter, but add that I was sent by Jane Maypole. The carer stares blankly at me, but Cherry dumps the tambourine on her snoozing neighbor's lap and totters toward me. It takes another two of my fifteen minutes, but eventually she stops an inch away from my face. I get a full-on whiff of old lady.

"Jane?" she croaks. "Jane Maypole?"

I nod and Cherry Butcher's scowl melts to a smile.

"Dear Miss Maypole."

We've made our way along the corridor to her room (another three of my minutes gone). Cherry Butcher's now sitting in another stiff-backed armchair by the window, a framed photo of a rather ugly man on the windowsill beside her.

I choose a footstool for a seat, then pull out my notebook and the *cherry red* Pip-Squeak (of course). By my internal clock we have ten minutes left.

"I looked after a fair few ladies in my time," Cherry continues. "But Miss Maypole was the peach. She was a troublemaker, you know. Used to have a good giggle about that, we did."

I make notes in my book.

- GAJ PEETCH
- TRUBBLEMAKER

Cherry Butcher glances at the ugly man on the windowsill and rubs one crooked hand with the other. "No one like her here, I'm sad to say. That bird you saw downstairs is the brightest spark, staff included." Her mouth resets in its thin, tight line. Then she sighs and almost (but not quite) smiles. "But enough griping. I have a visitor. What brings you here? We both know Jane is long dead, don't we, ducky?"

I explain about my family-tree project and that I need more information on how Great Aunt Jane died. "My family aren't being much help," I add, in case she's wondering why I'm bothering her.

But Cherry doesn't seem bothered. She shakes her head vigorously. "No, I don't suppose they are. Never were. Mabel was wild and Rose was off with the fairies." She taps her temple with a lumpy finger. "And all Fancy-Pants-Raymond wanted to do was boss Miss Maypole around, when he wasn't banging on about whatever masterpiece he was working on. Drove me to distraction, that one."

I nod and smile and write down her opinion of Raymond. Underline it. Twice.

- <u>BOSSee</u>

"But you want to know how she died, you say? Well . . ." Her eyes blur and I hold my breath.

"She had cancer, poor thing," Cherry continues, at last. "She invited the family over to tell them about it."

The terrible news! I scribble CANSA down in my notes.

Cherry waits for me to finish, then carries on. "But I think they was all having so much fun, she decided not to spoil things with her news. And the next morning she was dead."

She opens her mouth to say more, but we're almost out of time. I need to get to the point. "It was the cancer that killed her, not a crime?"

"Crime?" Cherry Butcher sits bolt upright in her chair, her eyes as bright as the parrot downstairs. "Oh, there was a crime all right."

I hold my breath and try not to look too keen.

"I've never told anyone, but since you're asking and all . . ." She leans forward in her chair, neatens her skirt across her wrinkled knees and lowers her voice to a whisper. "I was going to tidy her up a bit, you know, after she died, but before the undertakers arrived. And when I got to the top of the stairs, *he* was coming out of her room."

I scooch forward on my footstool. "Who?"

"Fancy-Pants-Raymond, of course. Said he was saying goodbye, but I got this funny feeling. And when I got inside, the room was all cleaned up. And – write this down in your book, ducky . . ." Cherry Butcher leans forward, bony hands clutching her knees. "*All her diaries was missing.*"

"Missing?" My voice catches in my throat. Is this the clue I've been waiting for?

Cherry Butcher nods. "That's right. She never let them out of her sight, because she wrote down all the village secrets and didn't want the wrong eyes prying. Piled them up beside the bed in the spare room, she had, after she swapped beds with that poor girl, Mabel. I saw them when I brought up her bedtime tea. Anyway, reckon Raymond helped himself to his dear, dead aunt's diaries, so he could use all her stories about the village for plots for his books and make even more money."

She leans back in her chair, a satisfied smile spreading across her face.

"There's your crime. Mark my words. Raymond stole Miss Maypole's diaries."

## ★ SIXTEEN ★

# Uncle Lionel

SUSSPEKT: UNKEL LIYONELL
RELAYSHUNSHIP TO GRATE ANT JANE:
GRATE NEFFUE
AGE ON JOON 26TH 1973: 11

I make it back to the library with thirty seconds to spare. Then wait another twenty minutes for Auntie G. Apparently, she couldn't resist popping in to see her greyhounds.

Not that it matters. Cherry Butcher has given me plenty to think about. Great Aunt Jane had cancer – that was her terrible news. Great Uncle Raymond was spotted leaving the spare room after she died. And then her diaries, which she'd piled up beside the bed for safekeeping, went missing. Or got themselves locked in the spare-room wardrobe, to be precise.

Every bit of me tingles. For the first time, I have some sort of motive. *He killed her for her diaries.*

That night, I sprawl on the scratchy bedspread and reread my case notes. The evidence is really stacking up against Great Uncle Raymond. He was the last person in the spare room before the diaries disappeared. Which means he must have been the one who locked them in the wardrobe. Because, according to Cherry Butcher, he wanted to steal her secrets about the village for his plots.

But does it also mean he tore out her last words?

I hang over the edge of the bed and peer into the dusty dark where I've stashed the diaries. "Does it mean he killed you?" I ask them.

But if Great Aunt Jane is under there, if she knows the answer, she isn't telling.

With a sigh, I heave myself back up onto the bed. As Rachel Bailey keeps reminding me, there are two more witnesses to interview. Uncle Lionel and Grandma Mabel.

After my parents and Niko and Oli, they're my most favorite people in the world. Which makes it even weirder that they don't like each other. I can't remember the last time they turned up at the same family party. Grandma Mabel gets Christmas and Uncle Lionel has Boxing Day. Grandma Mabel comes for Dad's birthday and Uncle Lionel is always there for Mum's. I get two birthdays, one for each of them, so it's not all bad. And if they do accidentally turn up at the same event, one of them either suddenly remembers something frightfully important that they need to do, or they sit at opposite ends of the table or opposite sides of the room and act like the other one doesn't exist.

Weirdest of all, my whole family seems to think their relationship is totally normal and if I dare to ask questions, they call me nosy.

Anyway, none of this matters. Neither Grandma Mabel nor Uncle Lionel are very likely suspects. But proper detectives interview everyone who was present at the scene of the crime.

*Proper detectives . . .*

The bedspread suddenly feels wrinkly as well as scratchy. Uncle Lionel and Grandma Mabel both live in Hampstead. Even if I can miraculously get from St. Jude's Junction back to London before Grandma Mabel's party, how will I be able to work out the bus maps when I get there? Or, horror of horrors, take the Tube?

Not even Rachel Bailey can help me with escalators.


The next morning, I lie on the sofa with a bowl of Shreddies and watch *Scott and Bailey* solve a whole season of crime without once getting on the wrong bus or tap-dancing at the top of an escalator. I sigh and plonk my bowl on the sofa beside me. Grandma Mabel's party is only two days away, and I'll be very much Mizzy the *Un*marvelous if I can't tell them how I solved the mystery of Great Aunt Jane's murder all on my own and unmask the culprit.

Suddenly, footsteps thunder down the stairs, along with the thud of a soccer ball. There's a rattle of Shreddies in the kitchen, the fridge door opens and closes – and in a goalkeeper-worthy dive, Oli joins me on the sofa, bowl clutched in his massive hands.

"I'm free today, Miz, if you want to work on your *family tree*." He slurps a mouthful of Shreddies. "Watson and Watson, remember?"

Which is how I come to be sitting next to Oli on the number 332 bus later that day, heading toward West Hampstead.

I lean forward in my seat and chew my thumbnail. According to Oli, Uncle Lionel's house is really near the bus stop on Finchley Road. I haven't a clue, but Oli got us by bus from St. Jude's Junction to the station in the middle of nowhere. And he knew which was the right platform for London, so I think he's got things covered.

The train was just leaving and we leaped on board. Well, Oli leaped, I clambered. Then we both collapsed, giggling, in our fuzzy orange seats, as the fields slipped away behind us.

Maybe it was the clambering, or maybe it was the collapsing, but ever since we got on the train, it's been like old times. Oli even agreed to a game of who am I? (he kept choosing goalkeepers of course, and I couldn't guess any of them, but even that was sort of normal). And at Victoria, he bought me a Starbucks with his own money and he didn't tease me, or act all grown-up and superior when I thought I'd lost my ticket in the machine. Or when I insisted we take the bus, rather than the Tube, because of the escalators.

It's so like old times, I risk telling him right here and now on the bus about my interview with Cherry Butcher and her theory about Great Uncle Raymond and Great Aunt Jane's diaries. He is helping me, after all, and I can still be marvelous, as long as *I* solve the actual case, not him.

Oli frowns. "So you think my grandad read the diaries to get ideas for his books. And then he locked the diaries in the wardrobe."

I bite back a smile. "Exactly."

"Which means my grandad most likely tore out the message about the poison too."

My smile breaks free. There's a reason Oli makes such a good Watson.

Oli smiles back at me. "So, he's our prime suspect and we're hoping Uncle Lionel and Great Aunt Mabel can provide a bit more evidence."

*Our.*

*We.*

A lovely warm tingle spreads to the tips of my toes. Watson and Watson once more, we get off the bus in West Hampstead and head (so Oli tells me) in the right direction for Uncle Lionel's house.

But all at once, my feet slow. Will Uncle Lionel even be home?

Uncle Lionel is a teacher and in his school holidays, he works in an orphanage in Pakistan. He wears baggy pants and tunics and this fuzzy white woollen cap. His Hunza hat, he calls it. Apparently, it's made from real goat wool from actual goats that graze in the world-famous Hunza Valley (well, it's quite well known for having soaring mountains and shriveled apricots). He's promised he'll give me one – a hat, not an apricot – but I'm still waiting. With luck, today will be the day.

If he's home, that is. Never mind alerting the suspects, I should have phoned to make sure Uncle Lionel is actually in the country. Oli won't be quite such a kindly Watson if I've dragged him all the way into London and up to Hampstead for nothing.

But it's too late now. I lift my chin and try to make myself feel better by being all Rachel-Bailey-fabulous in my pretend new white Hunza hat. I'm pretending so hard that when Oli stops walking, I crash into him.

"We're here," he says.

I stare up at the house. The sooty-black terraces all look the same to me. There's a string of colored flags hanging in the front window of this house though, so it must be the right one. Something to do with Buddha, Uncle Lionel says.

Oli marches up to the front door and knocks. Tummy twisting, I stand beside him on the doorstep and wait.

And wait.

And wait.

Oli frowns. "Did you call to say we were coming?"

"Um . . ." My pretend Hunza hat vanishes.

Oli sighs, knocks on the door again, then – joy of joys – he falls inside as it swings open and Uncle Lionel fills the doorway.

Uncle Lionel is Great Uncle Raymond's son and Uncle David's older brother, but he couldn't be any less like either of them. They're all thin and pointy and Uncle Lionel is big, with round edges. And he's funny and chatty and he loves kids (and almost-thirteen-year-olds) and he never drones on about his masterworks or shuts himself away with train timetables.

Did I say big? Actually, he's huge. Like a mountain crossed with a rugby player, he's wonderfully enormous and solid and (most wonderful of all) not in Pakistan. He's wearing one of his floaty tunics and his baggy pants and his Hunza hat (of course), but it's not as white as I was just imagining mine to be. Finchley Road isn't the cleanest of places.

"Mizzy! Oli! What a fantastic surprise!" His lovely turquoise eyes crinkle and he sweeps us both into a hug, then sort of scoops us into the house and along the dark, skinny hall to the sun-filled kitchen.

A stinky sweetness catches in the back of my throat. Something is bubbling on the stove and the table is a mess of chopping boards and bowls and those things that look like little baseball bats but are actually for squishing food. Everything – including the peacock-blue tablecloth – is smeared with green.

You see, Uncle Lionel loves tea. Not the normal kind you get from the grocery store. He makes his own from the plants he grows in his back garden. One of my favorite parts about visiting him is choosing which herb or flower to make tea with, then choosing which teapot to put it in.

Uncle Lionel has teapots from all his travels, arranged on a huge black dresser in the kitchen: little clay ones with bamboo handles, silver ones with flowers and hummingbirds, and a tall brass one with a long, curved spout like a swan's neck. My very favorite is shaped like an elephant. It's pink and orange and lime green and studded all over with jewels, and you pick it up by the tail and pour tea through its trunk.

"It's a new recipe I brought back from Peshawar at Easter," Uncle Lionel explains. He stirs the pot on the stove and leans over for a deep sniff. "Meant to be good for hay fever." He sneezes three times in a row, grins and winks. "Maybe a little more coriander . . ." He grabs a handful of green from one of the chopping boards and sprinkles it into the pot. "But I'm forgetting my manners! What would you like to drink?"

"Chocolate mint," Oli and I say at the same time.

Uncle Lionel makes our tea in my elephant teapot and carries the pot, a jar of honey and three teeny cups with no handles into the garden on a tray. The garden is actually a concrete square, with a fence on three sides and the back of the house on the other. But you can't see the fence, or the house, or the concrete, because every bit of space is crammed with pots of sweet-smelling herbs and flowers. Against the back wall of the house is a sort of outside dresser, as huge as the one in Uncle Lionel's kitchen, except not nearly so sturdy. Instead of teapots and cups, this one's laden with even more potted plants.

Uncle Lionel sets the tea tray on a little wooden table in front of the plant-dresser and tosses us each a cushion – purple for me, pink for Oli. He sits cross-legged on an orange one, folding up surprisingly small for a rugby-playing-mountain. "I've rearranged a little since your last visit." He sweeps a giant hand toward the dresser. "Everything on here is fine for nibbling, if you feel like it. The lemon verbena is my current favorite – very good for indigestion and most people find it very calming. But stay away from Shady Corner."

Uncle Lionel points beyond the plant-dresser toward the shaded part of the patio. Two pots of leggy blue flowers with spooky hoods and a leafy green vine sprawl across the fence. He laughs at the look on Oli's face. "Only aconite and belladonna. Safe to look at, just don't eat them."

Uncle Lionel tips up my elephant and a steaming stream of minty-chocolatey liquid pours into each cup. It's only when I'm adding my fourth teaspoon of honey that I realize he hasn't asked why we've come.

"Uncle Lionel," I say, licking my sticky fingers and wondering if I can squeeze a fifth spoon of honey into such a tiny cup. "I'm doing a family-tree project for school."

"Oh yes," says Uncle Lionel. "Ma said you'd been to visit. She thought I might be next on your list."

Great Aunt Rose told him we'd visited? I glance at Oli and he raises an eyebrow. Interesting.

"My teacher wants us to do stuff on how our relatives died," I continue. "As well as how they lived."

It sounds more unlikely each time I say it, but Uncle Lionel smiles. "Cool! I might just steal that idea. Anyone particular you had in mind, Mizzy? Ma mentioned something about Great Aunt Jane."

"That's right," I say, as casually as possible. I reach into my bag for my notebook and find the *jelly-bean blue* Pip-Squeak to write with. "She had to . . . er . . . rush off before she could help. Do you remember much about Great Aunt Jane?"

"Dear Jane," Uncle Lionel says. "She made us lumpy sweaters and saved us all her stamps. And she was the one who first got me interested in plants and teas. She knew all these recipes and remedies, and she let me harvest her garden quite brutally and mess up her kitchen at Number One Church Lane whenever we visited. It was never the same after she died and we moved into the house. Dad never liked messes at home."

I nod, like this is all fascinating. "And you were there the night she died," I prompt. "I'm just wondering . . . was there anything odd?"

Oops. Oli splutters into his teacup, but Uncle Lionel sips his tea. "Ah yes, the *how they died* part . . ." He gives Oli a slap on the back, with a massive hand. "Well, I was only ten or eleven at the time, but I think she died in her sleep, didn't she?"

"There are . . ." I stir my tea, like I'm super interested in swirly, liquid things, "a few different theories."

"Really? Like, maybe someone helped her on her way?" Uncle Lionel lets out a long, slow whistle. He isn't smiling anymore, but he doesn't look scared, or in a sudden hurry to go out or make a phone call. "It's hard to believe anyone would have wanted her dead. No wonder Ma practically fainted when you asked her these questions."

"Oh, I'm not accusing anyone," I add quickly. Not yet.

"Of course not." Uncle Lionel laughs, but not in a smirky sort of way. He's much too nice for that. "A summer project for school, you say? Let me see what else I can remember."

Uncle Lionel studies a tall, bushy plant beside him and I take the chance to throw Oli a reassuring smile. Mizzy the Marvelous, totally in charge. He smiles back at me.

"Well, I do remember Great Aunt Jane invited everyone to her house," Uncle Lionel continues. "Mum and Dad and me and David. Your grandma Mabel too, and your grandpa Johnny. Johnny had one of those awful summer colds, poor thing. Coughed and spluttered all through dinner. Dad said he should have stayed at home."

I scribble quickly in my book.

- GRAMPA JONNee COFF

"David and I probably spent the afternoon in the garden," Uncle Lionel continues. "Davey hated being outside unless it involved trains, but for me, Great Aunt Jane's garden was heaven. The roses of course, and the lavender and salvias. And those pale pink poppies all around the edge of the lawn, like giant butterflies."

"Um, Uncle Lionel –"

"Sorry, Mizzy, you don't want a plant inventory. I'm not being much use, am I?"

He's not, but I force a smile. At least he's trying to help.

But all at once, Uncle Lionel sits bolt upright on his cushion. "Hang on a minute . . . I do remember something." He claps his giant hands on his knees, throws back his head and laughs. "Your grandma Mabel threw up all over the table."

# SEVENTEEN

## Grandma Mabel

SUSSPEKT: GRANMA MABEL
RELAYSHUNSHIP TO GRATE ANT JANE:
NEECE
AGE ON JOON 26TH 1973: 30 SUMTHING

"Well," Oli says, as we head back to the bus stop. "Uncle Lionel obviously didn't do it."

I glance over my shoulder. Uncle Lionel's prayer flags are fluttering in his front garden. Like Uncle Lionel, they don't fit at all with the London gray of Finchley Road.

Something about his story doesn't quite fit, either.

"Maybe not," I say. "I just have a feeling."

"What kind of feeling?"

"I don't know . . ."

"Brilliant, Sherlock," Oli grumbles. "Bloomin' brilliant."

I bite my lip. He did call me Sherlock, but not in a good way. And he's right, of course. Feelings don't solve cases. I need evidence, and nothing Uncle Lionel had to say was new. Great Aunt Jane wrote about Grandma Mabel throwing up, and I've lost count of how many people have mentioned Grandpa Johnny's cough.

Oli checks his phone. "My grandad is still our best bet. There's not much point interviewing Mabel. She's dottier than Mum's greyhound cup, Miz."

He's right, again. Grandma Mabel is terribly muddly. "But proper detectives interview every possible suspect."

Oli shrugs. "My point exactly."

"Every single suspect." I give him my most dignified Rachel-Bailey hard stare, but my chin wobbles. Does he mean I'm not proper, or that Grandma Mabel isn't possible?

"OK, OK, we'll chat to Mabel." Oli checks his phone again. "But it had better be quick. I need to get back for soccer."

So that's it. Soccer. I should have known.

I trail along behind him. From Uncle Lionel's, it's a short walk up Hampstead Hill to Grandma Mabel's. The street is lined with trees and the houses here stand all on their own and have Pip-Squeak-colored doors and their gardens overflow with roses and daisies and those enormous floppy pink poppies.

Finchley Road is far below us when we finally reach Grandma Mabel's house on Frognal Road. Oli waves his phone. "Ten minutes max, Mizzy."

It's not enough. I hurry through the gate in the honeysuckle hedge and along the path to the front door. It's the exact same shade of yellow as Grandma Mabel's hat.

"Hey, Miz!" Oli jerks his head toward the back garden. "Back door, remember?"

Of course, Grandma Mabel never answers the front door. Especially not these days, when she's getting so forgetful about stuff. So much for Mizzy the Marvelous. Cheeks burning, I follow Oli around to the back of the house.

Grandma Mabel is standing in the middle of the lawn, arms stretched out like an unscary scarecrow, a whole bunch of crows feeding from her hands. She's wearing her sun hat and one of her baggy dresses, with the large patch pockets for birdseed. A strap of her swimsuit is visible where her dress has slipped off her shoulder.

Is she really going swimming, or does she just think it's Sunday?

Oli grins. "Your suspect, Sherlock."

I resist sticking my tongue out at him and stride across the grass toward Grandma Mabel. She doesn't seem to notice me, but the crows do. As one, they swoop to the giant chestnut tree at the end of the garden and eye Oli and me like we're bad news.

Grandma Mabel follows their gaze and smiles. "Ooh lovely," she says. "Is it Sunday?"

"No, Granny," I say. "It's Thursday."

"Thursday? Lovely! I love Thursdays."

Oli mutters under his breath. "Marbles. Losing them."

Grandma Mabel reaches up to hug me, like I'm tall and willowy and Bailey-like. "Goodness me, Mizzy dear – you've grown since last Sunday! Now stand very still, with your hand out. That's right." She scoops another handful of seed from her pocket and lets it trickle into my open palm. "You too, Niko."

Oli rolls his eyes at Grandma Mabel getting his name wrong, but stretches out his hand. All three of us stand in the middle of the grass and wait for the crows to return. The first two land on Grandma Mabel's hat and she giggles like a little girl. Two more swoop and peck a beakful of seed from my hand. One lands on Oli's head, nearly hitting him between the eyes in the process. He squawks, then tries to look like he didn't. Grandma Mabel beams at us both. "Aren't Sundays fun?"

Oli bats at his crow, but I smile. "They're the best, Granny."

"Now, where has your father got to?" says Grandma Mabel. "He promised to mow the lawn before we swim. Stephen!" She turns and peers at the house.

Oli shoos his crow away and pats the outline of his phone in his pocket. I ignore him. I grab Grandma Mabel's wrist to stop her searching for Dad. "He'll be out in a minute, Granny." I reach into her pocket and pour a little more birdseed into each of her hands. My own arms are aching, but she's still scarecrow-strong – because of all her swimming probably. "Can I ask you a few questions, while we're waiting? I'm doing a family tree for school."

"What sort of a tree, dear?"

"A family one."

"Ooh lovely," says Grandma Mabel. "Two of my favorite things in one."

"I need to know about Great Aunt Jane," I say quickly, to keep her on track and to hide the sound of another Oli groan.

"Jane, you say?" I nod and Grandma Mabel beams. "Dear Aunt Jane. Such a mother to me. She taught me everything I know about birds and gardens. I used to help her with her roses in St. Jude's Junction. Now that was a proper garden. Not just roses, but poppies and the lilac tree, such a heady scent . . ."

It's like being back with Uncle Lionel. For two people who both love plants so much, it really is weird that they don't get along. "Do you remember how she died?" I interrupt.

"Died, dear?" says Grandma Mabel. "Who died?"

"Jane," I say patiently. "Jane Maypole. Your aunt."

"Ah, Jane. Dear Jane. Such a mother to me . . ."

"Miz," Oli hisses. "We have a train to catch."

"Three minutes!" I hold up three fingers and try to look like his adored and adorable cousin, plus a hard-nosed detective rolled into one. Then I turn back to Grandma Mabel. "Do you remember the night Aunt Jane died? She invited you all to a party at St. Jude's Junction. She said she had something important to talk about." I'm leading the witness, but I'm running out of Oli's time. And patience.

It seems to do the trick. Grandma Mabel's turquoise eyes cloud over, like rain's coming. "It wasn't really a party. Aunt Jane invited us because there was some important news she wanted to tell us. Now, what was it?"

"Her cancer," I prompt.

"Cancer?" A crow lands on Grandma Mabel's hand and tilts its head. She searches its beady eyes. "I don't think she mentioned cancer. But Raymond and Rose were there, with their two little boys. Not that Lionel was ever a small child. He always looked five years older than David, not just one. But perhaps that was because David was premature? Or was it Lionel?"

Grandma Mabel's gaze drifts from the crow to the sky. For a moment, I worry she's floated off to wherever it is she goes these days, but then she carries on. "Jane's housekeeper cooked steak and kidney pie. Much too rich for me. I felt quite unwell and Jane put me to bed in her room – said I'd be more comfortable closer to the bathroom. She made do with that funny little spare room. And she dosed poor old Johnny to the gills with his ghastly cough syrup. Thick and red and sticky, it was. Tasted terribly of strawberries, he said. Or cherries. And then she shooed him to the couch downstairs, so he wouldn't keep me awake. Such a horrible chesty cough he had, poor thing. And the next morning . . ."

Her voice trails away and her eyes fill with tears. But I have one more question I need to ask. "Granny?" I ask gently. "Do you really think Great Aunt Jane died in her sleep?"

Grandma Mabel's head snaps back in my direction. "Died, dear? Who died?"

★ EIGHTEEN ★

# No More Time

As soon as we get home, Oli rushes off to soccer. Moments later, Auntie G swoops into the kitchen, plonks a takeout pizza on the kitchen counter and promises to play Clue when she gets back from the latest greyhound emergency.

As soon as she's gone, Niko appears in the kitchen doorway and sniffs the air. He peers in the box on the counter, helps himself to the largest slice of pizza with lime-green-nailed fingers (his hair is green now too), then slopes back through the kitchen and out the front door.

Uncle David, being Uncle David, stays shut up in my old room with his timetables.

I finish off the pizza then head upstairs and spend the evening sprawled on the scratchy bedspread in the spare room, reading and rereading my case notes. But other than Grandpa Johnny's ghastly red cough medicine, the trip to Hampstead and my two latest interviews have added zero new facts to the investigation. Zero new clues. Not even any red herrings.

I sigh and read through the facts for the gazillionth time. Great Aunt Jane threw a family party to tell everyone she had cancer. But everyone was enjoying themselves so much and then Grandma Mabel got sick, so she decided to save her news for the morning. By which time she was dead. Then Cherry Butcher saw Great Uncle Raymond coming out of the spare room and, when she went in to tidy up, Great Aunt Jane's diaries were missing.

I chew my Pip-Squeak. It's not enough, is it? But Grandma Mabel's party is on Saturday and I need to show everyone I'm Mizzy the Marvelous, not Mr. Bean. I need to solve the case.

I flip back through my notes one more time, until I find the family suspect tree. Then I study each face in turn.

Uncle David seemed rattled when I interviewed him, but he was only ten on the night Great Aunt Jane died, so he can't really be a suspect. I cross him out.

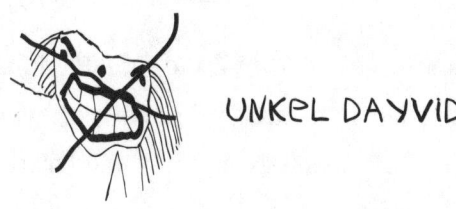

UNKEL DAYVID

Uncle Lionel was only ten or eleven, so he's probably out of the running too. Plus he was his usual lovely, helpful self when we visited and he really tried to answer all my questions. I cross him out too.

UNKEL LIYONELL

I add a quick sketch of Cherry Butcher then cross her out too. She might be rather grumpy and glarey, and she did cook dinner for everyone, so she could have added poison to the steak and kidney pie. But then more people would have died, wouldn't they?

CHERREE BUTCHA

I turn to the next face and smile. Of everyone I've interviewed, Grandma Mabel is the only one who got upset about Great Aunt Jane's death. Plus, like Oli says, she's dottier than Auntie G's spotty-greyhound cup.

She doesn't even really need a cross, but I give her one anyway.

Great Aunt Rose is a little more interesting. I chew my Pip-Squeak again. She didn't want us upstairs in her studio, definitely didn't want us looking at her portraits of Dad and Uncle Lionel and Uncle David, and she ran away as soon as I started asking questions about when the boys were born. But I never even *mentioned* Great Aunt Jane. So maybe she really is just cuckoo. I draw a question mark beside her.

Last but not least is Great Uncle Raymond. I bite my lip and peer at his pointy little face. Like Oli said, he's a bit of a fool and he's pompous and he likes his lamps better than he likes me, but proper detectives don't let that stuff get in the way. They focus on the facts.

Then again, the facts are piling up. I count them off on my fingers.

Fact 1. He went on and on about himself but shut up quick when I asked him about the wardrobe in Great Aunt Jane's spare room.

Fact 2. He said there weren't any diaries, before I even asked about them.

Fact 3. Cherry Butcher saw him outside the spare room after Great Aunt Jane died and just before the diaries vanished.

Fact 4. He's the only suspect with a motive. He might have stolen the diaries to use as plots for his novels.

Fact 5. Oli thinks he's guilty too.

A whole handful of evidence, but is it enough? I roll over onto my back and stare at the ceiling. Something is missing from my investigation and it aches, like a hole in my tummy. Even if Great Uncle Raymond locked Great Aunt Jane's diaries in the wardrobe, it doesn't mean he ripped out the missing page. And it doesn't mean he killed her.

I hug my knees to my chest and try to think like Rachel Bailey. She'd interview everybody again, wouldn't she? She'd look for more clues. She'd gather more evidence.

But I'm not Rachel Bailey.

I'm Mizzy the Trying-Really-Hard-to-Be-Marvelous.

And I'm out of time.

Great Uncle Raymond it is then.

Pulling out the *toy poodle* Pip-Squeak, I draw a big black circle around his head.

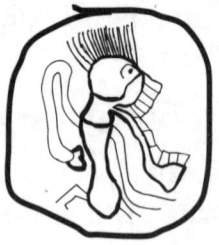 GRATE UNKEL RAYMUND

## ★ NINETEEN ★

# Unmasking a Murderer

It's Saturday morning and the smell of hot sausage rolls wafts through the house as Oli, Niko and I help Auntie G put the finishing touches on Grandma Mabel's birthday decorations.

A week ago, spending the whole morning with the boys like this would have been better than a whole new season of *Scott and Bailey*. And I'm super excited to see Mum and Dad. But mostly, all I can think about is Great Uncle Raymond.

My Rachel Bailey dress is hanging on the back of the door and I've swiped some eyeliner from Auntie G, and as soon as everyone's arrived, I'm going to tell them what he's done. How Mizzy the Marvelous worked it out all on her own. How no one needs to treat me like a baby anymore.

For the time being, I try to focus on balloons. Uncle David printed off an Excel table of which tube line colors to hang where. I ask him why, and he mutters something about Grandma Mabel always liking Underground trains. He actually looks me in the eye to tell me the yellow and green need to be twisted together for the District and Circle line between Tower Hill and Edgware Road. It's more attention than he's given me since I tried to interview him, so I'm not about to spoil things again.

I'm just finishing up the Piccadilly line in the kitchen when the doorbell rings. I hold my balloon breath. It can't be Great Uncle Raymond, not yet. I haven't got my dress on. I haven't done my eyes.

"Mizzy, darling!" Auntie G calls from the hall. "Your mum and dad are here! And the birthday girl!"

I heave a rubbery sigh of relief and join them in the hall with a mile-wide smile. "Hi, Mum. Hi, Dad. Hello, Granny."

Dad swings me in a circle and Mum swoops in for a hug. "Goodness me, sweetie. You've grown!"

Of course I've grown. I'm very-nearly-almost-thirteen and a successful detective. But I don't want to spoil the surprise. Not yet. I mumble about how many Shreddies I've been eating.

"Not too many, Mizzy. Your heart . . ."

I brace myself for the usual lecture, but luckily Mum is distracted by whisking Grandma Mabel into the sitting room before Uncle Lionel arrives. Apparently, Great Uncle Raymond is insisting that Uncle Lionel puts in a brief appearance this afternoon and nobody wants to risk Grandma Mabel missing out on her own party. Though to be honest, the way she is these days, she'll probably forget she doesn't like him and invite Uncle Lionel into the garden to feed the birds. Anyway, by the time Grandma Mabel has been safely stowed, Mum's forgotten all about my diet.

I tiptoe upstairs. It's time to slip into my dress, do wings for my eyes and add the finishing touches to my Unmasking a Murderer speech.

I slip my dress off the hanger, gather its slithery folds into my arms and carry it to the bed. Then wiggling and wriggling out of my hoodie and leggings and T-shirt, I slide the waterfall of midnight-blue silk over my head.

I hold my breath and turn to face the wardrobe mirror.

Mizzy the Marvelous sighs. Then she beams. Through half-closed eyes, in the old, mottled mirror, I look nearly-almost-lovely.

Knees-together-ladylike (instead of my usual crossed-legs), I kneel in front of the mirror and set to work with

Auntie G's *blackest-black* eyeliner (swiped or borrowed, depending on your point of view). The YouTube video made it look easy and I dab dots on one eyelid, join them together and fill in the swoopy outline.

Turns out eyeliner is not as easy to use as Pip-Squeaks, but when I sit back on my heels to admire my work, one half of my face looks more Rachel Bailey than I ever dared dream.

I lean in and start dotting the other eyelid, whispering my speech while I work. I'm just about to join up the dots, as well as the string of terribly difficult clues that led me to solve Great Aunt Jane's murder and identify Great Uncle Raymond as the culprit, when the bedroom door flies open and Oli barges in.

"Who're you talking to, Miz? And what's wrong with your eye?" He avoids the bed, but flops down on the carpet behind me, between the shopping bags and the shoeboxes.

"Nobody." I lean closer to the mirror and peer at my one swoopy eye. I should have 'borrowed' Auntie G's mascara too. My lashes are as short as my fingers. I bite back a sigh and join the dots above my left eye, trying my best not to wobble.

Oli watches me in the mirror, eyes narrowed.

My tummy tightens. "What?"

Oli gives his knuckles a long, slow crack. "Oh, you know. I just wanted to check you're not planning to scare my grandad half to death again." His eyes flick to meet mine in the mirror. "You're not, are you, Miz?"

I jerk to face him. "But you think he's guilty too. Don't you?"

Oli shrugs. Actually, he squirms. "Do I? Well, you know, yes, I suppose so. Not really."

"What does that mean?" My throat suddenly feels fat and tight, like one of Grandma Mabel's balloons.

Oli shrugs and smiles, all cheekbones and floppy fringe. "Come on, Miz. We had fun on Thursday. Watson and Watson and all. But I shouldn't have let it go so far. I should have brought you home after Lionel."

The wing above my left eye skids to one side. He shouldn't have let me go so far? He should have brought me home? What am I, his puppy? Sure, he wanted to get back for his soccer, but was he just playing with me all along?

I gulp at the balloon in my throat. "You don't believe me?"

"Well . . ." Oli scoops a half-moon of mud from his thumbnail. Flicks it onto the floor. "I believe *you* believe you."

My eyes prickle and burn. *I believe* you *believe you.* He was just playing with me, after all. "But it's true. You saw

Great Aunt Rose run away. You heard Great Uncle Raymond lie about the diaries."

Oli holds out his hands, palms up. "Yeah, but that doesn't mean he *killed* anyone. Come on, Miz. It's just a game . . ."

A game? He might as well have slapped me. Gathering up the folds of my dress, I stumble to my feet, barge past him and pound down the stairs. I'll show him this isn't a game. I'll show everyone.

The hall is suddenly crammed with people. Mum and Dad and Auntie G, and now Uncle Lionel, Great Aunt Rose and Great Uncle Raymond, like summer carol singers frozen in the open doorway. Everyone is here. My stage is set. As I march down the stairs and reach the bottom step, every head turns in my direction. Every mouth drops open.

This is it. The moment I've been waiting for.

Brushing a speck of invisible dust off his green velvet shoulder, Great Uncle Raymond totters across the hall toward me. "Ah, young Mizzy," he says. "How is your little family tree coming along?" Tooth by tooth he smiles his too-wide smile. Finger by scrawny finger, he pats my head.

It might be the "little." It might be the pat on the head. But just like that, I lose it.

"There isn't a family tree," I yell.

Uncle David tumbles in from the kitchen.

"There never was a family tree!" I scream.

Niko looms in the sitting-room doorway.

"I've been interviewing you all!" I bellow.

Oli thunders down the stairs. Shakes his head. Slices his neck with one finger. I turn my back on him. This isn't quite the speech I practiced, but it's definitely my moment – the one I've waited almost-thirteen years for.

"Somebody killed Great Aunt Jane," I say. "Someone murdered her. And I know who."

Mum grabs Dad's arm and gives him her here-we-go-again frown. Dad pulls out a what-am-I-supposed-to-do-about-it shrug. Uncle David taps a District and Circle line balloon with his burger-flipper, like he's testing it for leaks. Auntie G, Uncle Lionel and Great Aunt Rose stare up at me with lollipop eyes. Grandma Mabel cocks her head like a crow. Niko runs his green fingernails through his green hair and grins. Oli holds his head in his hands.

But the only person who matters right now is Great Uncle Raymond. I take a deep breath and lock him in my sights. "*You* poisoned her. You wanted her diaries to give you ideas for your plots, and you killed her!"

Chest puffed with pride, I wait for the cheers and awe and admiration.

What I get is more silence. Then more staring.

Then softly, quietly, Great Uncle Raymond begins to laugh.

He laughs and he laughs and he laughs. Then he claps. Then he congratulates Mum and Dad on my wonderful imagination. "Bravo, young Mizzy, bravo! I'm not the only storyteller in the family, after all." He splutters, he wheezes, he laughs again and when he's finally finished, he dabs his chin with his handkerchief, pats my head for a second time and looks around the hall, like he's the one making the speech. "Killed her for her diaries! I know we have our family secrets, but this one deserves the Booker! And whatever did she do to her eyes?"

My shoulders slump. My face flames. My whole, entire family is staring at me but not in the way I wanted. Like a wave, their laughter swells around me. Bigger, wider, higher. Until, like all the laughs that have ever been laughed at me, the wave crashes over my head and drowns me in one giant Ladies' Pond of water.

## ★ TWENTY ★

## Mizzy the Miserable

Apparently, almost-thirteen-year-olds *can* be left at home alone. Especially super-embarrassing ones who accuse elderly great uncles of murders no one believes even happened and who have to be driven home in disgrace.

Back in Putney the following morning, Dad gets home from work and goes straight to bed. I pretend to sleep, while Mum's morning noises – dishwasher, scraping toast and Classic FM – rise through my bedroom floor, along with the smell of burnt bread.

I crawl downstairs at the last possible moment. Mum repeats a long list of instructions (don't answer the door, don't answer the phone, don't eat matches or play with anything smaller than your mouth) and leaves for the hospital.

I make myself a bowl of Shreddies and mush them in the milk, so I don't choke to death by mistake, then settle down with Mr. Bean. Because let's face it – he's more my style than Rachel Bailey will ever be.

I botched my investigation (again) and even more stupidly (if that's actually, factually possible), I believed Oli was on my side. As Mr. Bean's theme tune fills the room, the TV screen wobbles and Grandma Mabel's party loops in slow motion before my eyes.

Laughter still ringing in my ears, I ran and shut myself in the downstairs bathroom. Dad, then Uncle Lionel, then Oli all knocked on the door and asked me to come out.

I didn't. Not for ages. I crouched on the floor in a soggy heap and wished I was as dead as Great Aunt Jane.

Unluckily for me, I wasn't. So, eventually, one eye streaked like that ink-blot test, the other blurred and red and puffy and even more squinty than usual, I rejoined the party and tried to look like I hadn't just made a complete idiot of myself and spent an hour in the bathroom crying.

I couldn't face the cake. The smell of the sausage rolls, which an hour ago I couldn't wait to eat, stuck to the back of my throat like barf. And every minute or so, the room fell silent, everyone turned in my direction and they all burst out laughing again.

The only person who didn't laugh was Oli. Somehow, that was even worse. He kept trying to catch my eye, his face all serious and sorry. But with every look, he sucked up another bit of that warm, tingly feeling from the bus when the two of us were heading off to interview Uncle Lionel, until all that was left was a big, empty ache in my heart.

And then Mum's laughter changed to crossness. Accusing strangers at the Ladies' Pond of stealing swiped-striped swimsuits was one thing, but accusing my own great uncle of murder? Auntie G tried to smooth things over. She even promised to spend less time with the greyhounds. But Mum had made up her mind. Apparently, me spending the holidays in St. Jude's Junction used to work when the boys were younger and *wanted* to play with me. But it isn't fair anymore. The gap between us is just too wide. Mum and Dad would make other arrangements.

I opened my mouth to object. I'm not a bunch of flowers. I don't need arranging. And what did she mean by *gap*? But the only words my lips could find were Oli's . . .

*I should have brought you home sooner . . . It was all just a game . . .*

I closed my mouth and while Mum carried on hissing and Auntie G patted her arm, I slunk outside to the car. A big, wide gap seemed really good right about now. Like the distance between St. Jude's and Putney.

Turns out, though, gaps are the worst. Turning off the TV, I pound upstairs to my room, stuff my head under my pillow and bawl. I want to be back in St. Jude's Junction, but not the St. Jude's Junction from this summer. I want the old one, when there weren't any gaps. When the boys believed in me.

But no one believes in me. Not even me.

I'm not even any good at crying. My sobs are loud enough, but the tears won't come. Dry-eyed, I crawl out from under my pillow and roll over onto my back.

My ceiling's covered with big swirls of plaster – stripy half-circles heading in all sorts of directions. When I was little, I tried to make pictures from the shapes. All I ever managed was a bowl of dog food. Like everything else about me, this doesn't appear to have changed.

I choke back another sob. Dog food reminds me of greyhounds and Auntie G. Which reminds me of St. Jude's Junction. And wardrobes. And diaries. And murder investigations. And parties full of people laughing at me.

I sigh and study my fingers instead. They're short and sticky and when I turn my hands over, I see the weird single creases on each palm.

I close my eyes. Mum and Dad are right. Oli's right too. I'll never be a proper detective. I'm just a big, dumb baby in a My Little Pony bedroom. My rug is patterned with ponies. So is my lampshade and duvet cover. My whole bed is piled high with them.

I swipe Pinkie Pie onto the floor, followed by Rainbow Dash and Applejack. I grab a handful of others and fling them at the wall. They make a surprisingly loud thud and I hold my breath. Have I woken Dad? But after a minute or two, Dad is still snoring. Which makes me feel sad and stupid and alone, all over again.

I slither off the bed and land face to face with yet another My Little Pony – my suitcase. Mum packed it for me yesterday while I hid in the car and I haven't even peeked inside yet. If I unpack, maybe I won't feel quite so useless.

With a sigh, I crawl across the floor on my hands and knees and unzip the suitcase. I toss out leggings and T-shirts. I rummage through socks and underwear. The pile of clothing on the floor grows higher, the suitcase grows emptier, until right at the very bottom, *MY AMAZING LIFE* shines up at me.

I bite my lip. What if, maybe, just maybe, there's a brilliant clue I've missed? Like the pages might burn me, I flick through my case notes.

- LUMPEE SWETERZ
- STAKE AND KIDNEE PY

I flick forward and backward, from color to color and clue to clue.

- COFF
- PUK
- MEDSUN

My Pip-Squeak scribble blurs. My eyes burn and my throat aches. Who am I kidding? Brilliant clues? My notes are more like one of those books I used to do with Grandma Mabel, where you join the dots and make a picture. Except, all my clues join up to is a stupid, straggly mess.

Mizzy the Total Failure hurls the journal into the corner of the room and torpedoes stupid little ponies on top of it. Until, one by one, her detective days are buried at the bottom of the pile.

★ TWENTY-ONE ★

# The Phone Call

The next day, at 9:23 a.m., the telephone rings and everything changes.

Mum always tells me not to answer the phone (I might drop it or strangle myself with the cord – never mind it's cordless) and eventually, it stops.

Then it starts again.

Then it stops.

It's probably someone selling something. Mr. Bean is in the middle of jump-starting his Mini with an ambulance so I don't think anymore about it.

But, just as Mr. Bean is posting a letter and getting stuck inside the mailbox, Dad staggers into the room. His hair is standing up in all directions and his eyes are gummed and bleary. I'm about to explain why I let the phone wake him (babies don't answer phone calls), but the look on his face stops me in my tracks.

"That was your auntie G," he croaks. "Raymond's in hospital. Some sort of poisoning, apparently."

Mr. Bean and the mailbox vanish, replaced by a rather-short-but-very-keen detective. "Poison?" I smile at Rachel Bailey, who is right beside me again. She smiles back and winks. I lower my imaginary six-inch lashes and wink back.

Dad looks at me with this really weird expression on his face.

"Poor Great Uncle Raymond," I say, closing my other eye in what I hope is a look of pain. "What happened?"

Dad rubs his stubbly chin and sighs. "No one seems quite sure."

"Hmm," I begin.

"Don't go there, Mizzy." He laughs, but his face doesn't look like he finds anything funny. "Why on earth would anyone try to poison Raymond? Much more likely he'd top *you* for that accusation you flung at him."

I can't keep my mouth shut a moment longer. "But Dad . . . don't you see? This means I was right! Well, I was wrong about Raymond being the killer, but I was right that *somebody* is. Someone poisoned Great Aunt Jane. And now they've tried to poison Great Uncle Raymond too!"

It's clear as glass to me, but Dad looks like he's peering through mud. "That's a bit of a stretch, Mizzy. The doctors think he drank his eye drops by mistake. It happens more often than you'd think. Atropine is deadly, if you take it in the wrong way."

"His eye drops?" I repeat. "Are they sure?"

"Well, yes," says Dad after a moment. "Mostly. As far as they can be. They're still running tests."

"I see."

Dad rubs his chin again. "What do you mean, *you see*?"

I rub my chin too. "Well," I say, picking my words carefully. Dad needs to see me as a brilliant detective, not his batty daughter. "Maybe it was a mistake. Maybe it wasn't. These things can be arranged, can't they?"

I was aiming for Dad's wow-you-surprised-me look and I think I got it – only not in a good way. He shakes his head. "I repeat, why on earth would anyone try to poison Raymond?"

This is the part I'm not so sure about. It's a fizzing tummy thing, and Dad's more the cold-hard-facts sort of guy. How can I convince him Great Uncle Raymond knew more about Great Aunt Jane's death than he was letting on, when I haven't a clue *what* he knew? "He was ever so cagey when I interviewed him . . ."

Dad sighs. "Ah yes, I was forgetting you interviewed everyone."

"But he was definitely hiding something!" I say. "He got all spluttery and scared and practically kicked us out."

Dad rolls his eyebrows – a talent he saves for times of extreme exasperation. "I'm not surprised."

"But he was scared, Dad, and he was angry! He didn't want me poking my nose in and –"

Dad cuts me off. "Of course he didn't want you poking your nose in and neither do I! The Great-Aunt-Janeing stops now, Mizzy. Raymond drank his eye drops by mistake. Understand?"

I stick out my chin. Of course I do – I'm not stupid. But my tummy knows Dad's wrong.

I just need to hunt down a few more dots, join them all together, and I'll understand why.

## Hunting for Dots

Great Uncle Raymond is in the hospital for a week. I'm not allowed to visit. But when he finally gets home from the hospital, Great Aunt Rose invites me along with Mum and Dad and Grandma Mabel to a family party at their house to celebrate his recovery.

Mum and Dad ban me from wearing makeup and make me promise not to mention Great Aunt Jane, or murder, and I nod and smile and say all the right things. But every bit of me is prickling with excitement.

This party is the perfect place for Mizzy the Still-Might-Be-Marvelous to reopen her investigation.

When we arrive, Great Aunt Rose shepherds us straight through to the dining room. The table, draped in white linen, is artistically arranged with finger sandwiches (palest egg mayonnaise, in white bread, of course), itty-bitty cakes with pearly-white icing and barely baked puffy pastry creations that are probably supposed to be one-bite, but look more like not-quite-nibbles. At one end of the table is a pile of white china plates and a stack of white napkins, and in the center, a vase of white lilies drenches the room with their scent and drowns the smell of the food.

Not that I intend to eat much – though I will enjoy smearing sticky fingers and lips all over those napkins. We're the last to arrive, and as Mum and Dad head into the kitchen to help Great Aunt Rose, I get straight to surveilling.

On the window side of the room, Niko is huddled (and hoodied) in a leather chair, fiddling with his phone. Wisps of purple hair curl around his hood and his nails are a lovely shade of mauve.

Auntie G is pointing through the glass at the roses in the garden. Beside her, Uncle David's forehead crinkles like he's listening to her (but he's probably thinking about trains).

At the table, Uncle Lionel is piling his plate with the puffy pastry things. His back is carefully turned to Grandma Mabel, who is attacking the itty-bitty cakes. This must be a family record – the two of them in the same house twice in ten days.

Oli (who didn't say hello to me and who I definitely didn't say hello to back) circles the whole table, studying the food like he's looking for something big enough to actually eat.

Very pale in an emerald-green velvet jacket today, Great Uncle Raymond wafts around the room, droning on to anyone who'll listen about his close call with death. He's obviously loving the attention and only occasionally remembers to grab hold of an at-risk lamp or shepherd me back to the middle of the room, where my hands can't reach the wallpaper.

Normally, of course, I'd tune him out. But today I'm all ears.

"They told me I must have drunk my eye drops and they are the experts, so I suppose they must be right. But it does seem exceedingly unlikely that I would make such a silly mistake." Great Uncle Raymond peers down his nose at each of us in turn, like he's daring us to disagree.

"Then I remembered that I was rather upset after Mabel's party." He clears his throat and turns his beady eyes on me. "Your little accusation rattled me, Mizzy, I must admit. It shook me to the core that my own great niece would think me capable of harming someone. Least of all dear Aunt Jane."

Every head turns in my direction. I study the puffy pastry bites like they're a Rubik's Cube that needs solving and try not to think about the last party I was at.

"Of course, I hid my upset well," Great Uncle Raymond continues. "But Lionel knows how sensitive I am. The dear chap traveled all the way down from London the very next day, with one of his little bottles of tea to calm my nerves. I always have a few sips at bedtime to help me sleep, but in my distress I must have muddled it up with my eye drops . . ."

Great Uncle Raymond's mouth is still moving, but my ears are filled with a sudden rush of sound that isn't laughter. My heart hammers. My hands turn to ice. And a joining-up sort of dot shimmers in the middle of the pastry thingies.

Not a prawn.

Not a raspberry.

A small bottle of Uncle Lionel's tea.

I tiptoe away from the dining-room table, creep through the arch to the sitting room (skirting the tallest, most expensivest lamp in the whole house) and curl up on the sofa in the corner. There's a blanket draped artistically over the arm and I pull it over my head.

I've brought my notebook and Pip-Squeaks in my schoolbag. Safe in my woolly cave, I take them out. There's not much light under the blanket (even though it's white), but I slide out what seems to be the *jelly-bean blue* Pip-Squeak and jot down my shiny new fact.

UNKEL LIYONELL BROOD SPESHUL
TEE FOR GRATE UNKEL RAYMOND

I stare at what I've written. But why would lovely Uncle Lionel poison his father? He's barely even a suspect for Great Aunt Jane's murder.

Or is he?

In the stuffy warmth of the blanket, I shiver. Heart thumping, I fumble through my notebook to the family-suspect tree and peer at each face in turn.

Great Uncle Raymond is out of the running for obvious reasons. I draw a cross over his circled head.

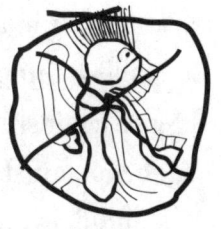

GRATE UNKEL RAYMUND

Uncle David too. He was even younger than Uncle Lionel when Great Aunt Jane died, so he almost certainly didn't kill her and wouldn't need to poison his father to cover anything up. Anyway, the only way he'd ever murder anybody is if he tied them up and recited train timetables at them. I trace over the cross I had drawn earlier.

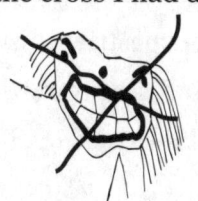

UNKEL DAYVID

Grandma Mabel isn't really a suspect, either, poor thing. I trace over her cross as well.

Which only leaves Great Aunt Rose and Uncle Lionel.

Great Aunt Rose got really rattled when Oli and I snuck upstairs and looked at the paintings of Dad and Uncle Lionel and Uncle David. And she ran away when I asked her about her family. Both these things are really weird, but there's no actual evidence against her.

But now there *is* evidence against Uncle Lionel. He made a special brew of tea and delivered it to his father's bedside. His own father, who later that very same night was rushed to hospital with almost deadly poisoning.

My tummy tightens. Uncle Lionel, my favorite of all uncles? Really?

I lift a corner of the blanket. Uncle Lionel is framed in the archway, standing on the far side of the dining-room table. He's still munching pastries, his Hunza hat slightly off-center, puffs of crumbs scattering down his tunic onto the pale wood floor. He looks nothing like someone whose attempt at murder has just been announced to the room.

I frown. I shouldn't have blamed Great Uncle Raymond for Great Aunt Jane's murder, just because I don't like him. So, I really can't rule Uncle Lionel out of the running for his father's poisoning, just because I like him best.

I can't erase the *X* I've already given him, but with trembling fingers, I lower the *toy poodle* Pip-Squeak to the page and add a big black circle around Uncle Lionel's lovely smiling face.

"Hey, Miz." Oli flops down on the sofa beside me.

I drop the corner of blanket and snap my notebook closed. But there's a tug, then a yank and the blanket yawns above my head as Oli ducks underneath to join me.

"Please let me see, Miz," he says. "Why did you circle Uncle Lionel?"

I give him my best Bailey side-eye. His face is shrouded in blankety twilight, so I can't actually tell, but he's probably just feeling sorry for me again. I keep my book and my mouth shut.

Oli inches closer. "Is it something to do with the tea he gave Grandad? Like, maybe Grandad didn't drink his eye drops?"

My heart gives the teeniest hop. He thought that too, huh? "Maybe not," I risk. "Everyone's just assuming he drank them because of the ankaleen."

"Atropine."

"That's what I said." I give Oli a full-on Bailey glare, which he probably can't see because we're hiding under a blanket. Hopefully he feels it. "Anyway . . ." I lower my voice and try to sound casual-but-confident. "What if the Atro-thingy was in the tea? Dad says it can be deadly if you take it the wrong way."

Oli swipes his phone and his face glows in the gloom. His eyes scan left and right. Quick. Curious. Lots of serious today, but no hint of sorry. If there is, he's hiding it really well. I sidle closer and lean my chin on his shoulder – just so I can read the screen too.

After a moment, he begins to read aloud. "*Atropine is a medication used to treat certain types of nerve agent and pesticide poisonings . . . blah, blah, blah . . . diseases of the eye and gastric ulcers . . . fatal if ingested . . . blah, blah . . . occurs naturally in a number of plants belonging to the nightshade family . . .*" He glances up from the screen. "Fatal if ingested. Sounds like it was the eye drops, Miz."

I bite my lip. Maybe. But . . . "What's a lampshade family?"

"Nightsh– Never mind." Oli taps at his phone again. Clears his throat and reads. *"Nightshades are a family of flowering plants . . . some . . . tomatoes, potatoes, peppers . . . are common food . . . some, for example belladonna, are highly toxic . . . "*

My tummy tightens. "Belladonna. The bush with the blue hoods. Which Uncle Lionel grows in his Shady Corner."

I lower the blanket. Uncle Lionel is still standing at the dining-room table, munching on pastries, the frame of the archway like a prime-suspect circle around his head.

"What if Great Uncle Raymond knew Great Aunt Jane was murdered?" I blurt. "And he knew who really killed her? And the murderer knew that he knew?"

I hold my breath. Sounds like a lot of knowing, when I say it out loud.

But Oli doesn't look at me like I'm a silly little baby who makes up mysteries to investigate and needs looking after and arranging. "And you think Uncle Lionel is the culprit? With belladonna from his back garden?"

I nod like a bobblehead.

"But . . ." Oli swallows. "His own *dad*?"

I open my mouth, then close it again. In the week since Great Uncle Raymond was poisoned, I've read and reread my notes till my eyes blur. I've rewritten the evidence in different colors and combinations. I've searched forward and backward and upside down for any clues I might have missed. And come up with nothing.

"Maybe . . ." I think out loud. "Maybe Great Uncle Raymond said something the night I accused him. Something that let the killer know he knew."

Oli shrugs. "All I remember him saying is that you deserve the Booker Prize for making up stories. Kind of true, Miz."

There it is again, the sorry in his eyes. I grit my teeth and scan the room for more joining-up dots. Proper solid evidence to send the sorries on their way again.

Niko, still fiddling with his phone, now leans against the windowsill. His hood is down and the sun glints through the glass so his hair shimmers like a purple halo.

Grandma Mabel has nodded off in the chair Niko was sitting in.

Back still firmly turned toward Grandma Mabel, Uncle Lionel has moved on to the little cakes, while Mum and Auntie G clear the trail of empty plates he's left behind.

Dad and Uncle David look like they're practicing cricket shots with Great Uncle Raymond. Or is it golf?

Actually, it doesn't matter. Someone else has caught my eye. Great Aunt Rose has drifted away from the others.

She's standing by the window, farthest away from Niko, and staring into the garden. She was all pink-cheeked smiles when we arrived, but now her face is gray and sort of caved in, like my heart when Oli feels sorry for me.

But it's not her face so much that's caught my eye, it's where's she's looking. Teacup raised in one hand, almost-but-not-quite to her lips, she's staring at her studio.

The back of my neck prickles. Great Aunt Rose's studio. The spiral staircase. The paintings of small boys who looked the same, which she didn't want us to see.

"Secrets," I say. "Family secrets."

The blanket slithers to the floor and I leap to my feet.

Then, with short, sticky fingers, I send the tallest, most expensivest lamp in the room crashing to the ground.

## TWENTY-THREE

# Joining the Dots

Halfway across the grass to the studio, a massive hand lands on my shoulder.

My heart stops.

I swivel around.

But it's Oli. Just Oli. "What are you up to, Miz?"

My heart restarts with a jerk. I peer past him, back toward the house, but no one else is following. Too busy cleaning up terribly expensive lamps, I hope.

"Secrets," I repeat. "Great Uncle Raymond said there were family secrets." I can hear him in my head at that awful party, laughing at me. *I know we have our family secrets, but this one deserves the Booker!*

"Never mind secrets, what about the lamp?" Oli says. "What was that, Mizzy?"

I lift my chin. "I was creating a distraction."

Oli's eyes widen. "A distraction?"

I nod. "I need to get into the studio. The secrets are something to do with the paintings of Dad and Uncle Lionel and Uncle David. The ones Great Aunt Rose didn't want us to look at."

Oli glances at the studio. His forehead crinkles. "Maybe we should come back later . . ."

My heart caves in like Great Aunt Rose's face. He doesn't believe me.

Oli sighs. "Come on, Miz. Don't make another scene. Let's help clean up the mess and think things through a bit."

I shake my head. "There isn't time. Uncle Lionel poisoned his dad because of the family secrets and the secrets are in the studio. I just know it."

Oli eyes the house. "But –"

"We've got to be quick. If we come back later, whatever it is, he'll have hidden it."

I hold my breath. Please let him believe me. Please don't let this end up like the first time I told him about Great Aunt Jane. "In or out?" I plead.

Oli cracks his knuckles. He glances at the house again.

The vacuum drones through the open window. Heads bob up and down beneath the windowsill and Mum, her

I'm-going-to-be-patient-even-though-I-don't-feel-it face all pinched and pink and shiny, beckons me back inside.

"Miz..."

"Fine," I say. "Suit yourself." And spinning on my heel, I storm across the grass to the studio.

I slam the door behind me and gulp a deep, steadying breath. Every bit of me longs to check if Oli's changed his mind and is racing after me, but there's no time. As soon as the shattered lamp is sucked up, Mum and Dad will hunt me down and drag me home again in disgrace. By the look Mum gave me, she's probably already on her way.

Anyway, who needs Oli? I can do this on my own.

Pounding through the middle of Great Aunt Rose's splattered rainbow, I scrabble up the winding staircase to the balcony. I have to squint and peer through the gloom, but as my eyes get used to the change in light, row after row of little boys stare back at me.

The paintings that Great Aunt Rose didn't want us to see. I step closer and tilt my head. The same three boys, over and over, with frowns and gappy grins and bony/chubby knees sticking out the bottoms of their gray school shorts. Great Aunt Rose is a very good artist and although they're all a bit square, the boys are obviously Dad and Uncle David and Uncle Lionel.

I tilt my head the other way. Or are they Uncle Lionel, Uncle David and Dad? Trailing my hand along the frames, I walk along the row, peering at each face as I go. Just like I remember, Uncle Lionel and Dad are impossible to tell apart.

I make my way down another row. And another. I grab each skinny, curly-haired, blue-eyed boy, tip him forward and check the name. Just like Oli did last time. Some are Dad. Some are Uncle Lionel. But, unless you read the names, you'd swear they were the same kid.

Now why is this important? I have to get this part right. Though I hate that Oli said it, I can't afford any more "scenes." I chew my bottom lip. Why would Dad and Uncle Lionel look so alike?

Because they're cousins?

No, that doesn't seem enough. I don't look a bit like Oli or Niko.

Oli and Niko look alike though . . . the same dark hair (when Niko's isn't dyed) and the same lovely brown eyes.

Hang on a minute. Not just my tummy, but my whole body starts to fizz, bubbling and spluttering like a volcano's about to burst through the top of my head. Oli and Niko look alike because they're brothers. What if Dad and Uncle Lionel are *brothers* too?

What if Dad is actually Great Aunt Rose's son, not Grandma Mabel's?

I feel like I'm getting closer. But Dad and Great Aunt Rose don't look a thing alike.

I stare at the pictures again. Uncle Lionel and Dad both have curly hair (what's left of it). They're both really, really tall. They both have blue eyes, like me and Grandma Mabel.

Grandma Mabel . . .

The truth hits me, like a crow between the eyes. I look like Mabel, because Dad looks like Mabel. Uncle Lionel looks like Dad, so he looks like Mabel too.

My head swims, my knees melt and I sink to the balcony floor.

If I'm not completely upside down and back to front . . . Grandma Mabel is Lionel's real mother.

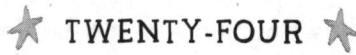

## TWENTY-FOUR

# The Elephant-Shaped Teapot

Grandma Mabel is Uncle Lionel's mother. This is some secret all right.

Through my hammering heart, I know one thing. No one is supposed to know. Uncle Lionel might have poisoned his dad just for *mentioning* family secrets at Grandma Mabel's party. But what has any of this got to do with Great Aunt Jane's murder?

I haven't a clue, but I bet Uncle Lionel does.

Mum and Dad hunt me down in the studio and, after making me apologize to Great Uncle Raymond and Great Aunt Rose and informing me (in stereo) that I'm grounded for the rest of the summer, they haul me straight home to Putney.

Dad pulls on his scrubs and leaves for work. Mum says she's pooped, then takes forever in the bath. When she's finally finished and her bedroom door closes, I tiptoe back downstairs and spend the night on the computer.

I pore over bus timetables and tube lines and google every map of London I can find. I pretend I'm Oli and Great Aunt Jane and Rachel Bailey rolled into one. And gradually, street by street, bus by bus, a plan takes shape.

Eyes gritty and crusted, mind a swirl of numbers, I'm ready to battle my demons.

The following morning, Classic FM and toast scraping waft up through my floorboards. Dad comes home at seven, the front door opens and closes again and Mum's Crocs flap down the path to the car. More Classic FM and more scraped toast, this time with some of those words Dad swears he never says.

Finally, it's Dad's turn for bed. When I'm sure he's had time to fall asleep, I get dressed and creep downstairs. Then, with only my notebook and Pip-Squeaks as backup, I tiptoe from the house.

Uncle Lionel needs another visit.

\* \* \*

Three hours and seventeen minutes later, I'm striding along Finchley Road, eight feet tall. I wasted an hour on a bus heading *down* the A3 highway rather than *up* it, and another forty minutes waiting for a number 16 bus instead of the 91, but somehow or other, Mizzy the Marvelous has made it to West Hampstead. Without using a single escalator. All on her own.

I brace myself on Uncle Lionel's doorstep, tummy fluttering in time with his flags. He takes forever to come to the door again, which might mean nothing. But as great detectives know, everything usually means something. Our job is to work out what's important and why.

Is Uncle Lionel in the shower? Is he boiling a kettle and can't hear the door? Much as it hurts to imagine him doing anything bad, is he burying a body in the back garden, beneath the belladonna?

Footsteps finally hurry along the hall and the front door swings open.

I almost topple over backward.

Uncle Lionel isn't wearing his Hunza hat.

Now, this seems very important. Uncle Lionel *never* doesn't wear his Hunza hat. But today, his head is pink and shiny and bare, with silver tufts sticking up on either side, like one of those monkey creatures at London Zoo.

"Mizzy!" he says. "What . . . are you doing here?" His hand flies to his head and he tries to smooth his tufts of hair.

I can't help it, I stare at his head.

"I can't find my hat," he says. He smiles, but his eyes don't twinkle like they usually do.

"Hi, Uncle Lionel," I say, trying to cover up the shock of his naked head, hold on to my opening line and imagine my dearest, kindest uncle as a killer, all at the same time. "I do mind . . . I mean, you don't drop . . . that is, I hope you don't mind me dropping by." I take a deep breath to steady myself for the upcoming masterpiece. "I just love having tea with you."

I rehearsed this line the whole way here (except when I was panicking about which way the bus was heading on the A3, or when I was trying to work out which way up sixes and nines go). It's meant to lull Uncle Lionel into a false sense of safety, before I blindside him with a tricky question, or ten.

But my opening, it seems, is not as brilliant as I hoped. Uncle Lionel's smile slips to one side and he joins me on the front step. He pulls the door closed behind him with a click and scans the street over the top of my head. "You're on your own?"

I nod. This seems to relax him a little. He looks back at me and almost smiles. "You made it here all on your own?"

I nod again and try to look like a person who regularly travels between one place and another and arrives at the right destination. Uncle Lionel's smile widens. "Tea, you said?"

"Yes, please, Uncle Lionel. With honey, please." I use my I'm-just-your-favorite-niece-who-likes-hot-drinks-made-from-plants-and-lots-of-honey voice.

Uncle Lionel's face softens like ice cream in the sun and he pushes the front door open again. "What's tea without a hiveful of honey, eh, Miz?"

Now, this is the point where Rachel Bailey would call for backup. Nobody knows where I am and Uncle Lionel might be a killer. But I don't have anyone to call. So, ignoring the fluttering lump in my tummy, Mizzy the Very Brave and/or Very Stupid takes a deep breath and heads through to the kitchen.

Somehow, even though the hall is as skinny as a string of spaghetti and Uncle Lionel is a rugby-playing mountain he overtakes me and reaches the kitchen first. He bulks himself out in front of the kitchen table, like he's trying to fill the space.

I try to look like I'm not peeking under his stretched-out arms. There's a pot of tea on the peacock-blue tablecloth – the brass one, with steam rising from its swan-neck spout – and sitting beside the pot are two small clay cups.

Two.

I sniff the peppermint-scented air. This is definitely important. Uncle Lionel was having tea. With another person. But who? Other than Uncle Lionel and me, the room is empty.

I want to pull out my notebook and Pip-Squeaks, but it's probably best to pretend I haven't noticed. I make a mental note (in *peppermint green*) and get back to my plan. Plonking myself down at the end of the table, I stare pointedly out of the window, away from the the telltale tea party.

For some reason, this makes Uncle Lionel even stranger. He leaps sideways from the table (a sort of *glissade*, if I remember my ballet lessons right) and lands beside the back door, where he spreads himself out across the window part like a starfish clinging to a rock. "I was just having tea . . . with someone," he stammers. "They had to . . . um . . . leave." He peers over his shoulder into the garden, turning his head from side to side, like he's about to cross Finchley Road in the middle of rush hour.

I swallow a sigh. To get Uncle Lionel talking about family secrets and poison and why he murdered Great Aunt Jane, he needs to be *relaxed*. But relaxed is the very last thing he seems right now.

I rock back on my chair and pretend to be fascinated by a dirty mark on the ceiling. This seems to do the trick. There's a rattle of cups, a gurgle of taps and the click of the kettle turning on. Eventually, Uncle Lionel sits down beside me.

I return my gaze to the table. The swan teapot and the two clay cups are nowhere to be seen and Uncle Lionel seems more or less normal again. Except for the missing hat and the shiny pink head. While the kettle boils, I prattle on about what I'm reading over the summer and quiz him about why adults think reading is such a great idea. This is the lulling part.

When the water's ready, Uncle Lionel brews tea in my favorite elephant teapot. I'm expecting to head out into the garden, like last time, like every other time I've ever been here (even when it's pouring with rain and he has to use the giant golf umbrella he keeps specially for rainy-day tea parties and he says it's just like the monsoon). But Uncle Lionel brings the pot and two silver hummingbird cups back to the table.

He pours a long stream of tea into one cup and pushes it across the table toward me. "Chocolate mint, your favorite," he says, nudging the cup closer. "Now, Mizzy, to what do I owe this delightful surprise?"

Uncle Lionel doesn't look delighted. Far from it. He's perched on the edge of his chair and his massive hands are pressing palm-down into the cotton tablecloth. Sweat stains darken the blue around each finger.

I cautiously sniff the tea while I stir. It smells like chocolate mint — but is it?

And why hasn't he poured any for himself?

I stare at the hummingbird on my cup. I stare at Uncle Lionel's lovely turquoise eyes. Then I take a deep breath and lift the cup to my lips. "Oh, you know," I say, taking a sip. "I was wondering why you looked so like my dad when you were kids."

For what feels like forever, we stare at each other like lopsided reflections in one of those wonky mirrors at the fair.

"I wondered when someone was going to notice," Uncle Lionel says at last, his voice all funny and hoarse. "I shouldn't be surprised it's you."

I risk another teensy sip of tea as Uncle Lionel stares out of the kitchen window. Definitely chocolate mint. "Is it because you share the same mum?"

Uncle Lionel sighs. He wipes his head with a sweaty hand and the pink gets even shinier. "Mabel is my birth mother," he says, at last. "She wasn't married when she had me, which was a big deal in those days. Or maybe she just didn't want me." His turquoise eyes cloud over. "As soon as I was born, she gave me to Mum and Dad. Your great aunt Rose and great uncle Raymond."

He fumbles for the hat he isn't wearing, then pats his tufts of hair, like he's wondering what they are. "Mum and

Dad took me in and pretended I was theirs. No one, including me, was supposed to know. But I never felt like I quite fitted. And, bit by bit, I started to piece the clues together. David's birthday was only eight months after mine and I looked far more like Auntie Mabel than Mum or Dad. I imagine you noticed the same things."

He reaches toward my elephant teapot and strokes a green and orange toenail on one of its feet with his finger. "It was a gradual realization really, until one day, just after my eleventh birthday, I asked Mabel outright if she was my mother and she said yes. She tried to be all lovey-dovey and make it up to me, but she'd given me away. Like a sweater she no longer wanted." His eyes blur with tears. "I was hurt and angry and, I'm ashamed to say, I wasn't ready to forgive her. Worse than that, I wanted her to feel my pain." His face reddens. "I was only eleven. I decided to give her a really bad bout of diarrhea."

I blink. "Diarrhea?"

"It should have been a joke," Uncle Lionel says wearily. "A really bad joke. The next weekend, we all went to stay at Great Aunt Jane's for the family party you asked me about last time. I collected poppy heads from the garden. Great Aunt Jane had taught me all about plants and I knew the seeds were full of fiber and would do the trick. What I didn't know is that they're also full of opium."

*Opium.* Sherlock Holmes joins Rachel Bailey at my side. "Like the drug?" The drug that can kill people if they take too much.

Uncle Lionel hangs his head. "You're smarter than I was, Mizzy. I only knew about the fiber. I brewed the seeds into a tea, and on our way to bed that night, I swapped my brew for Mabel's bedtime cuppa. Then I snuck along to the room I shared with David and waited for the chaos to unfold."

He rubs his forehead. "But nothing happened. I fell asleep and when I woke the next morning, I found out Auntie Jane had swapped rooms with Mabel and the poor old thing was dead."

*Of course.* My Pip-Squeak notes rearrange themselves in my head. Great Aunt Jane, Cherry Butcher and Grandma Mabel all mentioned the room swap, but I missed how important it was. I've had the wrong end of the investigation all along. Great Aunt Jane was never the intended victim. It was Grandma Mabel.

A tear wobbles down Uncle Lionel's cheek. "Great Aunt Jane was very old and no one was surprised she'd slipped away in the night. Only me and my conscience knew she hadn't died from natural causes. Well, I suspect David had an inkling. He must have noticed I was up to something that night, but he never breathed a word to me." He reaches one massive hand across the table. "I was just a kid. I didn't know that poppies were so dangerous. I was horrified when I found out and I confessed everything to Dad."

I cross my eyes and give my best puzzled frown. Like I haven't understood a single word. Which, actually, is sort of true. He tried to give Grandma Mabel diarrhea, but he killed Great Aunt Jane instead? With poppy seeds? Dad sometimes makes poppy-seed cake and no one ever dies from eating it.

Uncle Lionel slides his hand back across the table and tucks it in his lap. "Dad never told anyone. Not even Mum. And it seems he gave you the cold shoulder when you started asking questions. He knew I never meant to hurt Great Aunt Jane. Maybe he believed I'd punished myself enough as it was. Anyway, Mizzy, I promise I've been making up for my sins ever since. It's not me helping the orphans. It's the orphans helping me."

Sins. Plural. *Great Uncle Raymond and the eye drops.*

"Sin. Not sins," Uncle Lionel corrects himself. "I know Dad's little eye-drop incident seems in keeping with my MO, but it really was an accident." He lays a giant hand across his heart. "I would never dream of hurting him. Any more than I meant to hurt Great Aunt Jane."

I want to believe him, I really do. But he's just admitted to killing Great Aunt Jane. And to telling Great Uncle

Raymond all about it. I bet Great Uncle Raymond was protecting him, the boy he had always treated as his son. Great Uncle Raymond must have checked the spare room for evidence, found Great Aunt Jane's diaries, ripped out her last message about the strange-tasting tea, then locked the rest of the notebooks in the wardrobe.

No one suspected a thing. Until I wanted to hang up my beautiful new dress.

And accused the wrong person of murder.

And the wrong person mentioned family secrets.

My tummy hardens into a stone-cold lump. However much he says he didn't, however much I wish he hadn't, this must mean Uncle Lionel tried to kill Great Uncle Raymond.

Does it mean he's trying to kill me too?

I gulp. The tea tasted all right, but Rachel Bailey is screaming for backup. Even Sherlock looks worried. I need to escape. But Uncle Lionel is watching my every move.

"It really was just a stupid, terrible mistake," he continues. "I must have used too many poppy seeds. You do believe me, don't you, Mizzy?" He leans forward on his elbows, his face close to mine, something green and herby on his breath. "You know how stupid eleven-year-olds can be. I'm sure you did tons of dumb stuff last year."

My neck's as stiff as a pack of Pip-Squeaks, but I force

a nod. I did tons of dumb stuff, of course I did. Hacked buttons off my new winter coat. Froze at the sight of any escalator within fifty feet. Accused people of stealing borrowed swimsuits.

But I never, ever killed anyone. Even by mistake.

"What are you going to do, Mizzy?" Uncle Lionel's eyes narrow, like he's trying to work out what – if anything – I'm thinking.

I long to blurt out everything I know. To show my lovely maybe-killer uncle what I've worked out all on my own. But that might be my stupidest act yet. I stare at his sweet, kind face and try to make my own as blank as possible.

"This is a lot to process, isn't it?" Uncle Lionel says at last. He almost-but-not-quite smiles. "How about some honey in that tea, eh, Mizzy? You've hardly touched it." He pushes back his chair and crosses to the shelf where he keeps his honey collection. "I think we should have the special stuff today. From Hunza. It tastes like apricots, because the bees feed on the blossoms."

I feel cold all over. Is the *honey* actually the poison, not the tea?

Uncle Lionel sits back down at the table and adds two glossy teaspoons of maybe-not-honey to my cup. Whatever it is is so thick that he has to nudge it off the spoon with his finger. When he's done, instead of licking or sucking, he wipes his finger on the tablecloth and pushes my cup across the table toward me.

"Thank you, Mizzy. I feel so much better for telling you."

The tiny silver cup glints in the sunlight from the window. The hummingbird on its surface shimmers, like it's straining to fly away.

"And of course," Uncle Lionel adds, a slow, sweet smile spreading across his face, "you must do what you see fit with my confession."

My hands shake. Tea sloshes over the rim of my cup and drowns the poor little hummingbird. I stare at my cup. I stare at Uncle Lionel's honeyless one. I stare at the thick, sticky smear on the peacock-blue tablecloth.

Then all at once, from somewhere in the garden, there's an almighty, thundering crash.

## ★ TWENTY-FIVE ★

# The Yellow Butterfly

In the split second it takes Uncle Lionel to reach the kitchen window, I scramble from my chair, stumble down the hall and fling myself through the front door. Is he following me? Not daring to look, I lower my head and race full pelt down Finchley Road.

Where can I run to, where can I hide? The street is full of cars, but just when I need it not to be, the pavement is glaringly empty. There's usually a zillion people here, but right now there's just an old woman creeping along like a snail in glue and a gangly teenager in a hoodie handing out leaflets.

Heart thumping, I dodge the old woman and bat the sheet of paper out of Hoodie's hand as I run past. Hoodie throws me a filthy look, but there's no time to care. Any moment now, Uncle Lionel's ginormous feet will pound the pavement behind me.

At the corner, bent over and gasping for breath, I risk a peek back along the street. Uncle Lionel's flags are waving in the breeze in his garden, but there's no Uncle Lionel. Not yet anyway. Maybe I can jump onto a bus, before he catches up with me.

But the only bus is stuck behind a mile of cars, moving even more slowly than the old lady. And I can't just wait at the bus stop for Uncle Lionel to come and grab me.

Unless . . .

Unless I head in the wrong direction and wait at a different bus stop. My heart hops. That might confuse him.

I have no idea which is the right or the wrong direction for anywhere, but almost tripping over my own brilliance, I race back past the teenager, past the snail lady, past the waving flags, to the bus stop way beyond Uncle Lionel's house.

Even Rachel Bailey is struggling to keep up.

I flop panting and dripping onto the bus-stop bench.

I'm now even farther away from the creeping bus but if my plan works, I've bought myself a bit of time. Uncle Lionel will expect me to have gone the other way.

If he's following me, that is.

From where I'm sitting, I can just make out his front

door. It's wide open, but that was me, wasn't it? The garden, the front path and the street on either side of his house are empty. Except for the little old lady inching back along the pavement toward my bus stop, like her sense of direction is even worse than mine.

There are no rugby-playing mountain-men. No men of any kind. Even Hoodie has gone. The bus creeps closer. So does the snail lady. There's still no sign of Uncle Lionel. Why? Where is he?

I gulp a deep, calming breath, but my heart still hammers and my tummy flips and twists like a Slinky on a spiral staircase. All the evidence suggests that one of my most favorite people in all the world is a murderer. He tried to poison Grandma Mabel and killed Great Aunt Jane by mistake. Then, when Great Uncle Raymond accidentally gave away his motive for the first murder by talking about "family secrets," Uncle Lionel tried to poison him as well. And now he just tried to feed me poisoned honey.

Except . . .

My spidey senses are jangling. Something doesn't fit. If Dad uses different poppy seeds for his cake and there's another kind that can actually kill you, the rest is clear. A young boy, with an interest in plants, who had just found out who his real mother was. Add swapped rooms and wrong victims . . . and it all makes sense.

But if I'm right, then why isn't Uncle Lionel chasing me?

I chew my thumbnail, stare at my bus and try to make it move faster. Someone sits down beside me. Whoever-it-is is too close, especially in this heat, and I shuffle sideways along the bench, my eyes still glued to my bus.

The person shuffles closer. Closer. Until their feet touch mine.

Tiny feet in tennis shoes.

With scissored, frilly socks.

"Granny?"

Grandma Mabel is perched beside me on the bus-stop bench. Her breath comes in short bursts and under her hat (how did I miss her yellow hat?), her eyes flick left and right along the street. Like one of her crows, ready to fly away at any moment.

"Granny?" I pat her hand, but her eyes are blank. "Granny," I try again. "It's me. Mizzy."

Suddenly, Grandma Mabel focuses on my face and smiles. "Mizzy! Is it Sunday?" She squeezes my hand. "I'm in such a muddle. There's somewhere I'm supposed to be. Something I'm supposed to do. But for the life of me, I can't remember what." Her gaze wanders along the street again and her smile fades. "I don't suppose you could help me home, could you, dear?"

***

So now – instead of leaping on a bus and getting as far away as possible from Uncle Lionel, figuring out what to do about his confession and finding my way home to Putney, all before Dad wakes up – I'm half dragging and half carrying Grandma Mabel up Frognal Road.

Actually, I'm rather impressed with myself for remembering the way to Grandma Mabel's house. And now she's so forgetful, spending time with her always makes me feel clever. For a moment, I almost tell her what a brilliant detective I've been. That I've solved Great Aunt Jane's murder all on my own.

But poor Grandma Mabel seems even more muddled than usual today, and I don't want to stress her out more by mentioning Great Aunt Jane again. So I chatter about swimming at the Ladies' Pond instead and if this will be the week I manage without my water wings.

By the time we reach Grandma Mabel's house, I almost believe it's Sunday myself. I really should be getting home, but she invites me in for a glass of orange cordial and it's hot and I'm thirsty, so I follow her through the honeysuckle hedge, along the front path and in through her yellow front door.

I help her off with her sun hat, then feeling all Rachel-Bailey willowy beside teeny-tiny Granny, I reach up and hang it on the hook beside her Hunza hat.

Strange. I never noticed Grandma Mabel's Hunza hat before. Maybe she's been to Pakistan, as well as Uncle Lionel? I open my mouth to ask her about her trip, but Grandma Mabel has already scuttled through to the kitchen.

When I catch up with her, she's on her hands and knees, emptying out the cupboard under the sink. Behind her, the kitchen table is piled with dusty, sticky-looking bottles and jars, most of which look older than she is and seem to be almost or completely empty.

"I know I put it somewhere, dear." She pulls her head out of the cupboard and peers up at me, like I'm the last person she expected to see. "Mizzy? Is it Sunday?"

I bite back a sigh. She really is in a state today. "No Granny. It's Monday."

"Ah, Monday. That's right." She stares back into the cupboard. "Now, what was I looking for again?"

"Orange cordial," I say. "You're making me a glass of cordial."

"Am I?" Grandma Mabel ducks back inside the cupboard. Every so often she pulls out another bottle or jar, passes it to me, and I add it to the collection on the table.

I really should be going. My hands are even stickier than usual and Dad will be waking up any moment and starting a search party. "Granny?"

But Grandma Mabel is halfway inside the cupboard, rooting around at the very back. She probably can't hear me. I check the clock. If Dad oversleeps and has his usual forty-minute shower, and if I get lucky with maps and timetables, I might still be home in time. But I have to leave now.

"Granny," I try. "I have to go . . ."

"Here it is!" There's a muffled cheer from inside the cupboard and Grandma Mabel backs out, still on her knees, waving a small brown bottle above her head. She has the widest smile on her face I've ever seen. But then she looks back at the bottle and frowns. "What on earth do I want this for?"

"Cordial," I say. "You're making me a glass of cordial." The little brown bottle doesn't look much like cordial, but then half the bottles on the table are like stuff you'd only find in the British Museum. The one in her hand is probably just really, really old. Sticky and old. There's a grubby label with some kind of red fruit on it, so it must be what she's after.

"Ah yes, of course, dear. Some nice cordial." Grandma Mabel creaks to her feet and turns to face the sink. Like a slow-motion video, she takes a glass from the draining board, fills it almost to the brim with sticky stuff from the bottle, then adds a dribble of water from the tap.

I reach for the glass. But Granny doesn't let go. "I'm sorry, dear, I think this must be cherry." Her nose wrinkles. "It smells rather sweet."

"That's all right, Granny. I like cherry."

"Would you prefer orange?" She looks doubtfully at the pile of bottles and jars on the table. "Now, where will I find that?"

"Cherry's fine." I wrestle the cordial from her tight little fist and drain half the glass in one swallow.

Grandma Mabel opens her mouth. Then she closes it. She stares at the bottle in her hand. She stares at my half-empty glass. Then with a funny little crow-squawk, she grabs back the glass and empties what's left down the sink. "What have I done?"

For some reason, all I can think of is elephants.

Grandma Mabel pushes past me and hurries from the room. Am I meant to follow her? Possibly. Probably.

My legs wobble. I'd rather lie down and go to sleep, right here, but I zigzag after her. "Granny?"

She's in the hall, pinning her hat in place. Her floppy yellow sun hat, not that white one, floating above the coat rack like a cloud. She glances at me in the mirror, her face large and pale and rounder than I remember. Three small lines crease her forehead, exactly halfway between her eyebrows. Maybe she doesn't like the hat. I'm about to tell her to try that nice white one instead, when she scurries out of the house.

I stand in the doorway, swaying slightly. Or maybe the world is swaying around me? Grandma Mabel shimmers down the path and melts into the hedge, her hat like a giant yellow butterfly in the leaves. I like butterflies. And this one's huge. I stagger off the step, wobble down the path and follow it through the hedge.

Along the street toward the heath.

Maybe Grandma Mabel is going for a swim. After all, it is Sunday.

Swim . . . Suddenly, all I want is to slide into the cool green water of the Ladies' Pond.

"Hang on!" I shout after the butterfly. "I'm coming!"

## ⭐ TWENTY-SIX ⭐

# Uncle Lionel's Hat

Butterflies, honeysuckle and hats in the hall, hovering like puffy white clouds above my head. Am I dead? Am I dreaming?

When my crusted eyes open, instead of Grandma Mabel's hallway, a white ceiling stares back down at me. It's so bright, my eyes close again, without me having a thing to do with it.

I lie on my back for a bit and wait for the usual morning sounds. But instead of scraped toast and Classic FM, there's a screechy, squeaky bleep beside my pillow.

I peer at the ceiling again. No dog bowls. No My Little Pony lampshade.

I turn my head to one side. Everything's blurred, but bit by bit, a room takes shape around me. All white, except for some yellow roses in a plastic jug, on one of those tables on wheels. Next to the roses is a stack of Nancy Drew books – none of them mine – and a bowl of bananas, beginning to brown, just how I really hate them. Their sickly-sweet scent mixes with something bitter and chemical smelling.

Then next to the wheelie table, slumped at an odd angle in a very upright armchair, I spot Mum.

I croak her name, but she doesn't seem to hear me. Her mouth is wide open and a line of dribble creeps down her chin. I should wipe it away for her but, for some reason, my arms won't move, like all my parts belong to somebody else. They and the rest of my body are stretched out in the small, narrow bed. A hospital bed, maybe, with a ten-ton blanket pinning me in place.

But why am I in hospital? My brain rattles and echoes in a rattly, echoey way.

Am I sick?

Did I have an accident?

And what does any of it have to do with elephants, honey and hats?

The next time I open my eyes, Mum is staring at me. Dad too.

"Oh, Mizzy! I'm so sorry!" Mum's face is as white as the ceiling, her eyes red. "I knew I shouldn't have left you alone all day."

"She wasn't alone." Dad reaches an arm around Mum's shoulder. If anything, he's even paler than Mum, his eyes redder. "I should have woken up."

I want to tell them everything's OK. I've actually done something ever so clever. I just can't remember what.

Mum's eyes brim with tears. "We could have lost you."

Dad nods. "We did lose you. For hours and hours. How on earth did you end up in Hampstead? And what was all that about elephants and hats?"

I open my mouth. But before I can find any words, everything goes black.

When I wake up next, Mum and Dad have been joined by a talking woman in a white coat. Mum and Dad, for a change, are both listening. I should listen too. This woman must be a doctor and she's probably explaining what I'm doing here.

The doctor has a lot to say and she uses a lot of long words. It doesn't help that my head is thumping like Oli's kicking a soccer ball around inside my skull. But I catch the odd word. *Unconscious. Codeine. Cough syrup.*

"Could she have drunk someone's cough syrup?" The doctor looks from Mum to Dad, then glances in my direction and smiles. Like I'm a toddler, or a dog, or a toddler-dog.

She looks back at Mum and Dad. "The nighttime stuff, with codeine?"

A nighttime cough? Now this rings a bell. But why?

I shake my head and try to clear the fog.

"Your mother has a whole cupboard of old medicines," Mum says, turning to Dad. "Could Mizzy have got into that?"

Dad frowns. "I don't think so. I mean, Mum has a ton of old stuff. But how on earth would Mizzy have got to her house, all on her own?"

"Well, she was in Hampstead . . ."

Dad laughs. "Which means she was probably aiming for Brighton!"

The doctor studies me a moment, then turns back to the grown-ups. "Well, however she came by it, Mizzy had a good deal of codeine in her blood. Not enough to kill her, luckily, but she will be very woozy for a while."

My forehead throbs. My brain aches. My eyes close again.

Codeine . . . Cough syrup . . . Cherry-tasting cordial . . .


The next time I surface, the doctor and the bananas are gone, and Mum and Dad are deep in conversation with Uncle Lionel.

I'm pleased about the bananas and Uncle Lionel. I'm even more pleased that Oli has stopped playing soccer in my head and I can keep up with what everyone's saying. Even better, their words actually make sense.

I shouldn't let them see I'm listening, though. Especially not Uncle Lionel. I just don't remember why. I close my eyes and give a little snore.

"Someone found her unconscious in the street and phoned for an ambulance," Mum explains to Uncle Lionel.

"They took her to the Royal Free," Dad adds. "Then transferred her to Great Ormond Street, when they noticed her Down syndrome."

"Poor love." Mum's hand is cool on my forehead. "We never should have left her to her own devices."

"Poor love," Uncle Lionel agrees. "And . . . er . . . we don't have a clue what happened to her?"

"Not a clue," Dad answers. "God only knows how she ended up in Hampstead."

There's something about the silence that follows that makes me open one eye. Uncle Lionel is staring at Dad, blushing to the dome of his shiny, bald head. He's doing a really good impression of me doing my impression of a goldfish.

His shiny, bald head . . .

I squint and will my woozy brain to wake up. If only I had my notes.

My tummy lurches. My notes. Where are they?

Who's read them? I must remember to find them, as soon as I can move.

"Hampstead?" Uncle Lionel is now attempting an impression of someone completely disinterested in his own question. I forget about my notes and open my other eye. "They found her in Hampstead?" he adds, as if to underline how little he cares.

"Yes," Dad answers – much more patiently than I would. "She was on her way to the heath, by the look of things. Not far from Mum's place."

Lionel's head turns even pinker. He glances in my direction.

I meet his gaze.

Lionel almost hits the ceiling. "Mizzy!"

"You're awake!" Mum and Dad chime in, in true detective style.

I don't bother to answer them. I'm too busy watching Lionel squirm. Every bit of him turns red and beads of sweat roll, one by one, across the top of his naked head.

His.

Naked.

Head.

"Your hat," I mumble.

Lionel's hand jerks to his head. "My hat?"

"Your Hunza hat," I say. "It was at Grandma Mabel's. On the hook by the door."

"You were at Grandma Mabel's?" Mum and Dad look from me to Lionel and back again.

"Yes." Slowly things are coming back to me. "I helped Grandma Mabel home and Uncle Lionel's hat was hanging in the hall. She invited me in for orange cordial, but it tasted like cherries."

Mum looks at Dad. "So, you actually went to Hampstead on *purpose*, Mizzy?"

"Yes." My chest puffs a bit. I weakly turn to face my uncle. "And before that I went to Finchley Road on purpose too. Visiting Uncle Lionel."

Uncle Lionel turns as white as the blanket on my bed.

He stands and rushes from the room.

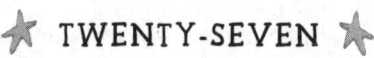
TWENTY-SEVEN

# Sorries

As Uncle Lionel rushes out, Auntie G sweeps in, followed by Niko and Oli. Auntie G scoops me into a ginger-biscuit hug and the boys hover awkwardly at the foot of my bed. Two sets of sorries in their eyes.

"That was odd," Mum says.

"What was odd?" Auntie G asks.

"Lionel . . ."

"He did seem in a hurry," Auntie G agrees. "Did he lose his hat?" She hugs me tighter and strokes my hair. "But never mind him. How are you, Mizzy? We were all so worried."

Just like that, it's like old times. Auntie G and Mum analyze the challenges of keeping their children safe. Dad nods off. Niko and Oli forget about feeling sorry for me, flop down on the end of my bed and pull out their phones. And I'm left pinned like mush beneath a blanket even a baby could kick across the room. How on earth did I imagine I could chase after Uncle Lionel, solve Great Aunt Jane's murder and prove myself to anyone?

But I *have* to chase after Uncle Lionel. I'm still mad at Oli for not believing in me and thinking I make scenes and for all the sorry in his eyes, but he's my only hope. I stare at the top of Oli's head and will him to look up.

He doesn't.

I clear my throat. Mum shoots me a concerned glance, but Oli doesn't flicker.

I smile reassuringly at Mum and try to kick Oli. But someone's stolen all my bones and neither foot reaches anywhere near him.

Then, all at once, Oli lowers his phone and sidles along the bed toward me. I'm about to hiss that I need to talk to him, when he leans down and hisses at me instead. "I need to talk to you, Miz."

I nod as enthusiastically as a mushy blob pinned beneath a baby blanket can and try to look casual, all at the same time.

Oli frowns and shakes his head. "Not here," he adds in a low voice.

Right. No. Of course not. Niko's mauve-nailed fingers are busy with his phone, but he's well within earshot. Auntie G has moved on from parenting children to looking after greyhounds, but Mum can listen to a whole room of people, plus the phone, all at the same time, and still know exactly what I'm up to and why.

"Fancy a ride in a chair, Mizzy?" Oli asks, at full volume.

Odds are, I can't even sit in a chair without sliding into a squishy puddle on the floor. But with every ounce of strength in my mashed-potato body, I nod.

Mum's head jerks in our direction, but Oli is out the door and back with a wheelchair before she can open her mouth. By the time she's actually making words, he's piled me into it and is wheeling me from the room, with promises to be back in five minutes and not a moment longer.

As soon as we're outside the room, I croak, "Uncle Lionel's going to poison Grandma Mabel. We've got to stop him."

"Shh. Not here." Oli wheels me along the corridor and safely through the double doors at the end of the ward.

"He killed Great Aunt Jane," I carry on, as the doors swing shut behind us. "It should have been Grandma Mabel but they'd swapped rooms. He's going to try again."

Oli pushes me along another corridor, toward the elevators. "Er, Miz . . ."

He doesn't believe me again, does he? Feeling a bit stronger, I twist around in the wheelchair, but I can't quite see his face. "It's true. I promise. He confessed it all. Then he tried to poison me with special honey."

We've reached the elevator and Oli reaches over my shoulder and presses the down arrow. "Actually, Miz, I don't think you're making it up," he whispers. "Not anymore. But let's wait for a bit of privacy."

I bite my lip. There's no time for waiting. No time for privacy. Uncle Lionel is on his way to kill his mother, Grandma Mabel. Right now.

The elevator dings, the doors open and Oli wheels me inside. I keep biting my lip and wishing I didn't need Oli or a wheelchair. After what seems like forever, the doors shut again. Oli presses the big, shiny G and the elevator sinks in sealed-in silence. In the mirrored walls, we're finally face to face.

Oli's cheekbones are as pink as my water wings. "You left Great Aunt Jane's diaries under the bed," he mumbles into the neck of his hoodie. "After what you said about Uncle Lionel and the tea, I had a proper look at her last entry and there's no way it's your handwriting. Much too small and neat." He meets my eye in the mirror. "Sorry, Miz. I should have trusted you."

Now, this is the sort of sorry I like. But as my heart melts to a puddle of porridge, the elevator jerks to a halt, the door opens and Oli wheels me through a wall of waiting people into the jam-packed lobby.

"Quick," I say. "Let's go!"

"What? Where?" Oli looks around the huge, rainbow-colored entrance hall.

"Grandma Mabel's!"

"You're in a chair –"

"It has wheels!"

"You're in a hospital gown –"

"Give me your hoodie."

"Your mum'll kill me –"

"I'll kill you sooner."

Oli glances over his shoulder, like he's weighing up the odds.

"In or out?" I hiss.

This time (wondrously, gloriously), Oli doesn't hesitate. "In." He pulls his hoodie over his head and drops it in my lap.

I smile. "Now wheel me to the ladies' room."

## TWENTY-EIGHT

# Mizzy, One Watson and an Escalator

Like all female detective shows, great endings begin in the ladies' room.

Oli waits outside, while I totter into a cubicle, lean against the closed door and wrestle my jellyfish arms into his hoodie. It hangs past my knees – not exactly Rachel-Bailey elegant – and my feet are bare. But at this point, who cares? We haven't a moment to lose.

I wobble back out into the lobby and flop into my wheelchair. "Let's go!"

Oli doesn't waste a moment. He scoots me across the lobby, through the massive sliding glass doors and out onto the street. Horns and sirens swirl around us and bounce off the towering stone buildings and Oli leans down, his mouth next to my ear, so I can hear him above the din. "Grandma Mabel's?"

I nod. There's no time to catch a bus, and anyway, the traffic is gridlocked. Which means . . . our only hope is my worst nightmare. I swallow hard. "On the Tube."

Oli looks at me like I've grown an extra head. "But Miz, you're terrified of the Tube."

I attempt a shrug. "I used to be. I'm older now. Maybe it's different."

I must sound braver than I feel, because Oli doesn't argue. He wheels me to the closest Underground station and as he studies the map and picks out our route, I gulp down a mouthful of barf.

But instead of an escalator, Oli pushes me to the elevator. Apparently, Russell Square is one of the oldest tube stations in London and they don't have escalators. Who knew? Maybe, our luck is changing and we'll catch up with Uncle Lionel in the nick of time.

We reach the platform just as a train pulls in. Oli heaves me and my chair into a surprisingly empty carriage. There's an old man asleep in the far corner and two teenage boys are sharing a bag of vinegary-smelling chips, both plugged into one phone. They clock my bare feet but as soon as they see my face, they look away. The tinny beat of their music rattles along with the train.

"OK," Oli says. "Tell me everything."

"Uncle Lionel's hat was hanging in Grandma Mabel's hall," I begin.

Oli nods. Then he shakes his head. "I don't get it."

Neither do I. But my bones – which are feeling stronger every minute – do. "Everyone knows he doesn't like Grandma Mabel. He actively avoids her. But he must have been to her house because his hat was there. And I think he'd brought her to his place. There were two cups on his kitchen table and he kept checking the back garden, like someone was hiding out there. And there was a gigantic crash like someone knocked his plant stand over. And then she was waiting at the bus stop on Finchley Road when I was trying to escape."

Oli shakes his head. "I still don't get it. Why would Uncle Lionel want to kill your gran?"

"Because she's his mother!"

Oops. That came out louder than I meant it to. The teenagers are lost in their music, but the old man opens his eyes, stares blearily in our direction.

I lower my voice. "That's why we couldn't tell Dad and Uncle Lionel apart in Rose's paintings. Why she didn't want us to look at them. Dad and Uncle Lionel are *brothers*. It was meant to be a secret."

Oli's forehead crinkles, then he nods. "But then Great Uncle Raymond let the cat out of the bag at the party, so Uncle Lionel tried to poison him. And now he's going to have another go at poisoning Mabel? But why?"

"Because she abandoned him," I hiss. "I don't think she wanted to, but he feels abandoned."

At our stop, Oli heaves me off the train, takes a moment to read all the signs, then wheels me down the platform toward the elevator. But a sheet of paper is taped to the elevator doors with big black Sharpie letters. *Out of Order*.

My tummy flips and falls. So much for good luck.

Using time we haven't got, Oli wheels me back along the platform and through the arch marked *EXIT*. As we come out the other side of the tunnel, I swallow a mouthful of barf.

The only way out is on an escalator as high as the Shard.

A surge of people sweep around us and onto the towering monster like it's the easiest, most natural thing in the world to do instead of the jaws of death.

I clutch the arms of my chair with cold, sweaty fingers. The ground around my chair shudders like the pretend earthquake at the Natural History Museum. The monster's metal teeth yawn and rattle and groan. The top of the escalator isn't even visible from down here, but I know all too well what's waiting for me – a terrifying tap dance, as the steps flatten out and fling me to the floor.

That's if I make it to the top without falling.

If I can bring myself to even step on board.

Oli stops pushing. "We could just head back to Russell Square, Miz. Get a bus . . ."

Across from the tunnel we just left, there's an archway leading to the southbound line. Oli's right. We could just head back to where we started. Back to the hospital, even.

I bite my lip. Maybe I've got the wrong end of the stick, like everyone always says I do. Maybe Uncle Lionel isn't racing to Grandma Mabel's house to kill her. Chances are, back at the hospital, Dad will still be asleep, Niko will still be on his phone and Auntie G will still be telling Mum all about greyhounds. No one will have even wondered where we are.

My fingers relax slightly. Through the arch there's a glimpse of lovely, flat, easy-to-get-to track and beyond the track, at the other end of the line, a nice, safe elevator is waiting for me. Great Ormond Street probably even has internet and we could watch some *Scott and Bailey* on YouTube.

Except . . .

My stomach tightens. I haven't got the wrong end of the stick. I know I haven't. Grandma Mabel needs me.

Which means (another mouthful of barf) I have to get on this escalator.

My heart pounds in my ears. Another train arrives and commuters stream out of the tunnel around us.

"It's OK, Miz," says Oli. "You don't have to do this . . ."

But I do, don't I?

Who else even knows that Grandma Mabel needs saving? Who else can save her?

The cough syrup has finally worn off, I think. With a deep, juddering breath, I heave myself out of the chair and inch my bare, frozen feet toward the escalator. The steps stream and clank and grind and while a vaguely familiar scream echoes around my ears (is it me?), I fling myself on board.

Oli leaps up behind me and I lean against him. Gulp breaths of metal-tasting air and try not to think about what happens at the top. But in no time at all, the steps flatten out.

I freeze.

I tap-dance.

I totter backward.

The upside-downing begins.

Then, all at once, I'm shoved onto solid ground and Oli tumbles over me, forward-rolling to his feet in impressive goalkeeper style. Tugging his socks off and shoving his sneakers back on, he puts his socks on my feet so they aren't totally bare on the hard floor of the Underground.

Then he takes my hand and together, Mizzy and Watson, we ignore the open-mouthed stares and wide-eyed whispers and totter toward the exit.

## TWENTY-NINE

# Cherries

Uncle Lionel's Hunza hat lies squished in the middle of Grandma Mabel's hall, a massive footprint stamped in its fluffy white middle.

Oli's socks are ruined so I drag them off, add my own gap-toed print to the hat and stagger through to the kitchen. Maybe the cough syrup hasn't worn off yet, after all.

Uncle Lionel is leaning against the table, his turquoise eyes all red and puffy.

"Where is she?" I totter past him to the back door. Crows dot the lawn, but there's no tiny, friendly scarecrow in a floppy yellow hat. I turn and glare at Uncle Lionel. "What have you done with her?"

"Nothing . . ." Uncle Lionel stammers.

Oli strides to my side and grabs my hand. "Then what are you doing here? Mizzy told me everything," he adds fiercely. "She worked it all out on her own."

For a moment, I gaze up at him, heart bursting. But there's more working-out to be done. I swivel back to Uncle Lionel and try to steady my voice. "Where is Grandma Mabel?"

Uncle Lionel spreads his massive hands. In one palm, like a crumpled butterfly, there's a yellow sticky note. "She says she's going to the police station."

"Ha!" Not very Rachel Bailey, but so what? I lift my chin. "She's going to hand you in!"

For some reason, Uncle Lionel's eyes bubble with tears. "No, Mizzy. She's handing *herself* in. She says she should have done it years ago."

I don't understand.

Oli drops my hand. I feel his eyes on my face, but I can't bring myself to peek. "Mizzy? I thought you said Uncle Lionel was the killer."

A moment ago, my heart was bursting. Now it's stopped dead. "I did. He is. At least, I think he is . . ." My tummy twists. How did I get this so wrong? Uncle Lionel confessed to *everything*. He poisoned me because I knew he was a killer.

Behind Uncle Lionel, Grandma Mabel's kitchen table bows with the weight of all her bottles and jars. Ancient jars. Sticky bottles. Sticky, cherry-flavored bottles.

Cherries. "Cough medicine . . ." I murmur. "With Copeen . . . feen . . ."

"Codeine?" Oli asks.

Missing dots shower down behind my eyes. "Grandpa Johnny had a cough . . . he had horrible, cherry-tasting cough medicine. Granny made me cordial . . . but it wasn't cordial . . ." I gulp. Oli's hand finds mine, our fingers frozen like ice. I look up at Uncle Lionel. "Grandma *Mabel* poisoned me?"

Uncle Lionel's eyes swim. "It must have been a mistake, Mizzy. You know how muddled she gets. She wanted to get rid of the old cough syrup. She was convinced it was proof of what she'd done . . ."

Pip-Squeak notes swirl and tumble, along with Great Aunt Jane's last words on the missing page of her diary. *My tea tastes like ch . . .*

Cherries.

Cough syrup.

My tummy lurches as the final dot falls into place. "Grandma Mabel killed Great Aunt Jane."

## ★ THIRTY ★

# The Ladies' Pond

"**G**randma Mabel killed Great Aunt Jane with cough syrup," I repeat, working out the clues as I speak. "Cough syrup has codeine. The doctor said that's what was in my blood. That too much codeine can kill you . . ."

I grab the sticky note from Uncle Lionel's hand.

*I am going to hand myself in. I have put it off far too long. But there's one last thing I need to do first.*

*One last thing she needs to do first* . . . What can it be? Uncle Lionel and Oli are watching me, like I'm the one with the answers. And the weird thing is, I finally realize they're right. I'm the one who knows this kind of stuff. Not Sherlock. Not Rachel Bailey.

Sticky-fingered, short-legged me.

Following the feeling in my tummy, I stumble back through the hall, over Uncle Lionel's hat, and out the front door.

Oli races after me. "Where are you going?"

"The Ladies' Pond," I call back over my shoulder. "Grandma Mabel's gone to the Ladies' Pond."

Weaving and wobbling, I lead the others along the street and on to the heath. Dry grass slices my bare feet, my legs are jellyfish, and if it was any other moment in my life, I'd sag in a heap and refuse to budge. But it isn't any other moment. It's right now. And I have to find Grandma Mabel.

But my head is fuzzy and muzzy. Where on earth are the ponds? I turn one way. Then the other. Then back in the first direction. The sweep of grass is dotted with people throwing Frisbees and drinking coffee in the sun like this is just a normal day, but my tummy loops and twists, like one of those tennis balls being whacked around a pole. Have I gone the wrong way?

There's no time to think. I pick a direction and run. And once again, my tummy gets it right. The Shard comes into view on my right, just where it should be, and gradually the grass begins to narrow, until eventually, wonderfully, the woods close in around us.

A familiar path appears between the trees, a glimpse of water at the end. I pant toward it, Oli and Uncle Lionel glued to my heels. Past the Floaty-Boat Pond. Past the Fishing Pond. Past the Save-the-Birds Pond. Until, just as my jellyfish legs are pooling around my ankles where Oli's socks used to be, we reach the Ladies' Pond.

I lean, gasping, against the gate. "Wait here," I tell the others. "Men aren't allowed. I'll yell if I need you." And before they have a chance to argue, I push through the gate and totter as fast as I can, past the changing rooms toward the water.

The pond is silent except for the birds and the drone of the bees. A duck glides through the smooth green surface. The scent of roses hangs heavy in the air. And far out, in the distance, Grandma Mabel's yellow hat bobs up and down as she swims toward the middle of the pond.

One last swim, before she hands herself in.

Not if I can help it. Grandma Mabel's swimming bag is at the end of the dock. As I tiptoe out to join it, Grandma Mabel waves and glides through the water toward me. At the end of the dock, she stops and treads water, squinting up at me from beneath the brim of her hat.

I don't want to spook her. Not till she's safely on solid ground. If she has a bad reaction to anything I say, there's no way I can jump into the water and save her.

I take a deep breath and try to curve my lips into a calm, everyday, we're-just-hanging-at-the-pond sort of smile.

"Ah," Grandma Mabel says. "You know."

So much for having a bad reaction. Grandma Mabel seems calmer and more with it than she's been in months. She pulls herself up the ladder and perches beside me on the dock. "I wondered if you'd be the one to find me out, Mizzy," she says. "You sense things most people don't even bother to notice." She reaches for my hand, turns it over in her lap and studies my creased palm. "You remind me of Jane, that way."

On any other day, I'd bask in this warm, fuzzy feeling. Now, I shiver. I have to stop her from handing herself in, but how can I reassure her that she's done nothing wrong? Because if she's done what I think she's done, it doesn't get more wrong.

"What happened, Granny?"

"Well." Grandma Mabel drops my hand and hugs her skinny arms across her chest. Her swimsuit seeps cold water against my thigh. Her yellow hat hides her face. "I haven't a clue what day it is, Mizzy, or what I ate for breakfast. Did I even eat breakfast? But some things are burned on my brain."

What things? What exactly did she do? The sun slips behind the trees. Butterflies and midges jerk across the deep, green water. The fish beneath our feet gaze up at us with wide, hungry mouths.

"I didn't mean to kill Jane," Grandma Mabel whispers, at last. "I meant to make her sleep. So she couldn't give away my secret."

Ah. The secret. I know this part of the picture. "Uncle Lionel."

"That's right, dear," Grandma Mabel continues. "When I was young, a few years older than you, I had a baby. But I didn't have a husband." She sighs. "These days, nobody minds really. But back then . . . such disgrace. Such shame. My parents would have disowned me. But dear Aunt Jane took me in and she helped me hide my terrible secret. And when my beautiful little boy was born, I gave him to Raymond and Rose. Only the four of us knew the truth. That he wasn't actually their son – he was mine."

In the distance the ice-cream van tinkles. Grandma Mabel cocks her head for a moment, like she's listening to a badly tuned radio. Then she stares back down at the water. "It was the most painful thing I've ever done. But somehow I coped. I almost made myself believe I'd never had a baby. Until eleven years later, Jane invited everyone to dinner and said she had something terrible to tell us."

Another dot shimmers on the surface of the water. The picture is almost complete. "You thought she was going to tell your secret . . ." I say.

Grandma Mabel's hat makes one slow nod. "I panicked. Of course, Lionel had guessed who I was by then. He had asked me outright about it just the week before, but the poor boy was so upset and he didn't want to hurt Rose, so I was almost certain he wouldn't tell anyone. Not for a while anyway. But Jane – well, everyone knew how much Jane loved to gossip. I had spent the last eleven years waiting for her to give me away."

She sighs, rippling the water with her breath. "I had only been married to darling Johnny for ten months. I was terrified he would leave me if he discovered my disgraceful past. And I had just found out I was pregnant with your father, Mizzy. I couldn't bear the thought of losing another baby. I didn't know what to do.

"Jane didn't make a peep all through dinner. I decided she was saving my secret for breakfast." Grandma Mabel takes a deep, juddering breath. "So, that night, I slipped some of Johnny's cough syrup into her bedside tea. The heavy-duty stuff, full of codeine. I thought it would make her oversleep in the morning and we could all be gone before she woke up. And my secret would be safe, at least for a while. Then perhaps, later on, I could talk her out of telling everyone."

Grandma Mabel dips a toe in the water. Circles spiral across the pond, like one dot leading to another. Grandpa Johnny had a terrible cough . . . he was taking heavy-duty cough medicine . . . which tasted like cherries . . .

Grandma Mabel pats my thigh, her fingers like icy twigs. "So, Mizzy dear, it was an accident, but I killed Jane. Her death was all my fault."

But another circle fans out across the pond. One that Grandma Mabel can't see, doesn't know. My tummy fizzes. "Actually, not quite," I say.

Grandma Mabel's hand stiffens on my leg. "What do you mean? I poisoned her. With Johnny's cough syrup. I didn't mean to, but I did."

My words tumble out in a rush. "Uncle Lionel added crushed poppy seeds to your bedtime cup on the very same night. He'd found out you were his real mum, remember? Just before Great Aunt Jane invited you all to her house? He was so hurt you had given him away and he wanted to hurt you back. He was trying to give you diarrhea, but Great Aunt Jane was in the spare room, not you. So *she* drank the poppies. *And* she drank the cough syrup you added to her tea. Opium and codeine."

I count off a finger for each deadly ingredient Great Aunt Jane had drunk. "And she had cancer. It was all too much for her."

"Cancer?" Grandma Mabel jerks to face me.

"That was the terrible news Great Aunt Jane wanted to share with you all," I whisper. "Not your secret."

Grandma Mabel's turquoise eyes darken. Shimmer and ripple like the pond. "Oh, Jane . . ."

I squeeze her skinny fingers. "But don't you see?" I say. "This means nobody murdered anyone. Not you. Not Lionel. It was all just a terrible accident." My tummy fizzes. I've worked it out. There's no way Grandma Mabel will hand herself in now.

But Grandma Mabel bites her lip. "I knew about Lionel's poppy seeds. He told me years ago, after he returned from his first lot of traveling, and decided to forgive me for giving him away. He was nineteen or twenty then. We've met every week since." I stare at her.

"Always in secret, of course," Grandma Mabel adds. "I never wanted Johnny to know the truth about my past and Lionel, dear boy, was always so loyal to Rose. He was terrified she'd think he liked me best. So we made a big show of not liking each other at all. And of course, our *real* relationship was the reason poor Jane ended up dead, and we never wanted anyone to connect us over that."

Another circle spirals across the pond toward me. "But I guessed." I swallow. "So you tried to poison me . . ."

Grandma Mabel's head jerks toward me. "Oh no, Mizzy, no. I'd never hurt you. Lionel warned me that you were on to us. That it was only a matter of time before someone believed you. We were just having tea, planning how to keep our terrible secrets safe. But then you showed up on Lionel's doorstep and I panicked. I convinced myself that Johnny's old cough syrup was proof of what I'd done to poor Jane and all I could think about was going home and getting rid of it.

"So when Lionel let you in the front door, I ducked out the back. But I got tangled up in that giant plant stand and knocked the whole thing over and by the time you met me at the bus stop, I was in a terrible muddle. Then you helped me home and I got even more muddled. And you said I was looking for cordial when I was looking for the old cough syrup so I could get rid of it – and before I knew it, I'd given you a glassful of the ghastly stuff."

My heart gives a hopeful hop. Nobody tried to poison me. Nobody murdered anyone. Everything's going to be all right.

But Grandma Mabel sighs. "Your parents are right, dear. I should be locked up where I can't cause any more damage."

She gazes out across the pond. A bird is still singing somewhere in the trees, but the bees are silent and the shadows have crept across the water toward us. "Poor Jane's death was both our faults, but I was the grown-up. Lionel was just a child. It absolutely wasn't his fault. And," she continues, "if I can take the blame for what happened to poor Jane and protect my darling boy at the same time, well . . . it might go a little way to making things up to him. And to her. I should have handed myself in years ago."

I grab her hand. "No! You can't. You mustn't."

"Oh yes, dear, I must." Grandma Mabel's tiny hand is stronger than it looks. She tugs free of my grip, scoops up her swimming bag then scurries back along the dock. "And I better get a move on, before I forget what I'm doing."

## THIRTY-ONE

# The Saver

"No! Granny. Wait!"

A care home is one thing, but prison? Dad would never recover. And what will it do to our family if it comes out that Great Aunt Jane was really, truly killed? By two of her very own relatives?

My tummy twists and twists and twists, until I can hardly breathe. Oh, why didn't I think things through, before I stuck my Mizzy the Oh-So-Stupid nose into other people's business? I scrabble back along the dock.

"It was an accident," I shout after her. "And you're both so sorry . . ."

Grandma Mabel pauses at the end of the dock. She slides her bag off her shoulder, pulls out her towel and dries herself down. She wriggles her frock over the top of her still-wet swimsuit, pulls on her frilly socks and slips on her tennis shoes. Then she shoulders her bag again and, yellow hat bobbing with every step, rushes on across the grass.

There must be something I can do to stop her. To save her. Like she always saves me.

*Like she always saves me* . . . My heart leaps. There is something I can do. If I'm brave enough to do it. I stare back along the dock toward the water. It's very dark and very deep and I don't have my water wings. I'll sink like a stone, I know I will. And Grandma Mabel will have to save me. Like she always promises she will.

Without pausing to pull off Oli's hoodie, I pound back along the dock and hurl myself into the pond.

Weeds grab my ankles.

Water floods my ears and my eyes and my nose.

Darkness tugs at my toes.

But I don't fight it.

Gasping a last lungful of air, I let the water drag me down. Down. Down. Down.

Until, sure enough, like every Sunday that I can ever remember, a birdlike arm loops my neck and Grandma Mabel tows me back to the safety of the reeds.

I blink and cough and gasp for air. Water trickles from one ear. Pond weed slithers from the other. But who cares? My plan worked! Grandma Mabel saved me, so I saved her.

My teeth are chattering and every bit of me is dripping, but I can't stop smiling. Even when we join Oli and Uncle Lionel on the other side of the gate and Grandma Mabel orders them to look the other way, peels the soaked hoodie over my head and drapes Uncle Lionel's floaty tunic-shirt around my shoulders. Even when she buttons me up, with horrid, loopy-loose buttons.

"That was a clever plan, Mizzy," she breathes in my ear. "Sneaky, but clever. Just like Jane."

Somewhere in the distance, the ice-cream van tinkles. My smile widens. I earned a million ice-cream cones today. As we head back across the heath to Grandma Mabel's house, even though the grass prickles my bare feet, I'm walking on air. I'm Mizzy the Marvelous. A real, live, proper detective. I solved Great Aunt Jane's murder and I saved Grandma Mabel too. And I didn't need anybody's help. Not even Rachel Bailey's.

I'm so marvelous, in fact, I even notice Grandma Mabel is leading us the wrong way across the heath and suggest a different path.

I'm such a brilliant noticer, I see Uncle Lionel squeeze Grandma Mabel's teeny hand in his own massive, rugby-playing bear paw.

I see her lean her yellow-hatted head against his chest.

I even clock the lovey-dovey looks they sneak each other, when they think Oli and I aren't watching.

And to Mizzy the Marvelous, it all makes sense. Of course Grandma Mabel and Uncle Lionel love each other. That was the funny feeling I always got around them, wasn't it?

My smile stretches even wider. My tummy always knew.

Unfortunately, my tummy doesn't have a clue that Grandma Mabel isn't leading us home.

## ★ THIRTY-TWO ★

# Pip-Squeak Case Notes

My heart joins my bare feet on the pavement. Hampstead Police Station looks like my school – tall and red, with lots of arched windows for prisoners to stare out of and see what they're missing. Grandma Mabel takes one long look, then scurries up the front steps and disappears through the double swing doors.

Uncle Lionel, Oli and I scrabble to catch up. Our footsteps echo in the cavernous entrance hall and every head in the place turns to watch our race. Grandma Mabel in her floppy hat, her still-wet swimsuit leaking through her dress. Uncle Lionel in his ribbed vest and footprinted Hunza hat. Oli, at least, is more or less normal, but I tug Uncle Lionel's tunic toward my knees and hope against hope my bare feet aren't leaving gap-toed prints on the gleaming linoleum floor.

Grandma Mabel reaches the front desk first. If only there was a long line of newly arrested villains ahead of us. Maybe then I'd have time to change her mind. But there isn't a criminal in sight when we need one. Only a gang of police officers leaning against the walls. Watching us.

Grandma Mabel stands on tiptoe, peers over the top of the marble-rimmed desk and clears her throat. "Excuse me, officer."

To the policeman on the other side of the desk, her yellow hat must look like a droopy sunflower. He folds his shirt-sleeved arms across his chest.

Grandma Mabel stares up at him. She doesn't speak and, for a wonderful moment, I think she's changed her mind.

Wrong.

"I want to confess a crime," she says.

The policeman raises one thick, caterpillar eyebrow. "That's a new one," he says. "Most folk around here want to report one."

"Mabel . . ." Uncle Lionel's fingers wrap around Grandma Mabel's upper arm. If only it was her mouth.

Caterpillar-Eyebrows glances at Uncle Lionel. At his vest. At his footprinted hat. At his tufts of hair, sticking out sideways above his ears. Then he looks down at his computer screen. "When did this crime take place, ma'am?"

"Now, let me see . . ." Grandma Mabel shakes off Uncle Lionel's hand and tilts her hat to one side. "It was 1971. Or was it '72?" She glances up at Lionel. "When did I marry your father, dear? Oh, how silly. He wasn't your father, was he? Or was he?"

"Mabel —"

"Let's say 1972." She peers over the rim of the desk, as the policeman types. "Now, I expect you want the specific day, don't you? It was definitely summer. The lilac was full and frothy and the roses were coming into bloom. Aunt Jane did love roses, so did the robin, of course . . ." She pauses and tilts her hat to the other side. "But was it late June or early July? And was it Wednesday or Tuesday?"

Caterpillar-Eyebrows stops typing. "No need for the exact day, ma'am. What was the nature of the crime?" He looks up from the computer screen, his brows now one bushy line, much thicker than his narrowed eyes. "There was an actual crime, was there?"

My tummy tightens. Please let her have forgotten all about it again.

"Oh yes," Grandma Mabel says, sounding thrilled to know an answer. But then she frowns. "Or was there? I mean my crime was a crime, but the other crime was just an accident. Oh dear." She clamps a hand over her mouth and looks up at Lionel. "Have I said the wrong thing?"

Caterpillar-Eyebrows sighs. He glances at the group of police officers who have, at some point in the last few minutes, gathered behind us like kids in PE watching Judy Mitcham point out my weird feet. All five of them are grinning. The smallest policewoman presses her chin into her checkerboard tie and stifles a giggle.

My tummy relaxes a smidge. Perhaps it will be OK, after all.

Caterpillar-Eyebrows clears his throat. "So, the crime, or crimes, are fifty years old. Possibly more. With all due respect, ma'am – why are you reporting them now?"

It's Grandma Mabel's turn to sigh. "I'm not reporting them. I'm confessing to them. To one of them."

"Right, ma'am," said Caterpillar-Eyebrows. "Yes, ma'am. And what exactly are you confessing to?"

Grandma Mabel rises on the very tips of her tennis shoes and leans forward over the rim of the desk. "To murder," she whispers.

Caterpillar-Eyebrows frowns. "And who did you murder, ma'am?"

I hold my breath.

"Why poor Aunt Jane, of course!"

I open my mouth to stop Grandma Mabel, but Uncle Lionel beats me to it. "Wait a minute, Mabel." He turns to Caterpillar-Eyebrows and lays his giant hands on the marble desk rim, each thick, sausage finger spread wide. "I – I killed her too."

No! My tummy lurches. This is all wrong. What is he thinking?

Caterpillar-Eyebrows almost, but not quite, sighs. "Killed who, sir?"

"Great Aunt Jane." Uncle Lionel hangs his head, which must give the policeman a really good view of the footprint on his hat.

"Is that the same lady as Aunt Jane, sir?" says the officer. "Or is this another one?"

"The same. We both killed her."

Caterpillar-Eyebrows stares at the top of Uncle Lionel's Hunza hat. He glances at Oli. Then he narrows his eyes at me. "What about you, little girl? Did you kill this aunt as well?"

I clench my fists. Little girl? Every bit of me wants to show Caterpillar-Eyebrows and his cronies who I really am. To tell them Grandma Mabel is not a crazy old lady and that she really did kill Great Aunt Jane (by mistake and with a bit of help from Uncle Lionel) and that I – me, Mizzy the Marvelous – solved the whole case on my own.

But that's the very thing I mustn't do, isn't it?

I need to save her, all over again.

Stretching my eyes wide, I let my tongue slip out between my teeth and shake my head from side to side, like it's still bunged up with pond weed. "Oh no," I lisp. "But I squashed my pet spider once. Poor Uncle Legs . . ."

Caterpillar-Eyebrows opens his mouth. Then he closes it. Then he looks from Oli to Uncle Lionel and back again. "Whichever of you is in charge," he says at last, his eyes finally landing on Oli, "all props to you. Care in the community, and all. But wasting police time is another matter. Now, run along and take them all home."

My heart leaps. We've done it! I grab Oli's hand and Uncle Lionel tightens his grip on Grandma Mabel's arm.

I'm just daring to breathe, when Grandma Mabel slides her free hand into her swimming bag, rummages around in her wet towel and pulls out a notebook.

My notebook.

My Pip-Squeak case notes.

My tummy plummets to the floor. So that's where they got to.

It's damp and blurry from her wet towel, but Grandma Mabel places *MY AMAZING LIFE* on the desk and slides it firmly toward Caterpillar-Eyebrows. "Here," she says. "This will tell you everything you need to know."

The policeman reluctantly takes my notebook and turns to the first page. His eyes flick left and right. Now it's my turn to hang my head in shame. Me and my darn detective work. I've gone and ruined everything.

Caterpillar-Eyebrows closes the book and slides it back across the desk to Grandma Mabel. "Very pretty," he says, at last. "Very wet. And entirely illegible. Was it in English?"

Grandma Mabel pulls herself up to her full height. "Of course it's in English. They're my granddaughter's case notes. Her spelling isn't the greatest, but she's quite exceptional, you know. She's a detective, just like Aunt Jane. Tell them, Mizzy."

Everyone turns in my direction. Caterpillar-Eyebrows. His cronies. Uncle Lionel and Oli. Some eyes widen. Some narrow. But nobody speaks. Nobody laughs.

The silence grows and swells and seeps into the corners of the hall. And still, everyone looks at me.

This is the moment I used to dream about. My chance to show the world I'm not a baby. But my notes are ruined, aren't they? They might have been badly spelled to begin with, but now they are also *entirely illegible*. The officer said so. There's nothing I can do about that.

I take a deep breath, cross my eyes and smile. Keeping my eyes crossed, I snatch back my book and take Grandma

Mabel's hand. And while she babbles on about dates and crimes and robins in the roses, and Uncle Lionel and Oli look wordlessly at each other, I lead her back across the linoleum, through the double swing doors and down the steps to freedom.

## ★ THIRTY-THREE ★

# Mizzy the Pretty-Marvelous-After-All

It's the last day of August. School starts tomorrow and the whole family is in St. Jude's Junction at Uncle David and Auntie G's for the bank holiday barbecue. Even Grandma Mabel has torn herself away from the fish pond at her lovely new care home beside the heath.

It's the first time I've seen anyone (other than Mum and Dad) since being grounded for breaking out of the hospital without permission and returning rather wet. Luckily for me, they were too busy finding the right care home for Grandma Mabel to ask too many questions. And even with the ones they did ask, they didn't really listen to the answers. They were even too busy to make other "arrangements" for me. But I figured I'd got away with enough for the time being, so I just stayed put and dreamed about this very day, when we'd all be together again and I could finally tell everyone how clever I've been.

Actually, I've spent the last three weeks thinking about nothing else. I even imagined wearing my Rachel-Bailey dress today for the barbecue, so I'd look the part when everyone met their new cousin-niece-daughter-grandchild, Mizzy the Marvelous.

But for some reason I can't put a short, sticky finger on, my dress is still in the wardrobe at home and I'm wearing my usual leggings and hoodie. When the air cools with that end-of-summer chill, Auntie G calls us all inside for tea and cake in the sitting room. Uncle David pulls out his train timetables. Dad counters with the photo albums. And without a word, Uncle Lionel, Oli and I sidle back into the garden.

It's the first time we've been alone together since they dropped me back at Great Ormond Street Hospital. The first time we've talked about everything that happened. We huddle awkwardly in the dried-up poppy patch, warming our hands over the glowing coals of the barbecue, and try to make sense of it all.

"I get it! I get it!" Oli says when I finish recounting the full investigation. Then he shakes his head. "I don't get it. What's the part about the cough syrup again?"

"Sorry, Miz." Uncle Lionel takes off his Hunza hat and smooths his tufts of hair. "I'm not sure I got it all either."

I sigh and pretend like I mind, but inside I'm beaming. There's nothing us detectives like more than explaining how clever we've been.

When I've finished for the second time, Oli still shakes his head. Uncle Lionel laughs and ruffles Oli's floppy hair. "Never mind, Ol. We can't all be brilliant," he says.

"Now, Mizzy . . ." He turns to me and the laughter leaves his voice. "When are you going to tell the others?" He twists his hat in his massive hands. "*What* are you going to tell them?"

The sitting-room window of Number One Church Lane glows softly in the early evening dusk. Mum and Dad are leaning over the back of Grandma Mabel's chair, all three of them laughing at a photo in one of the albums. Niko (with his new blue hair and fingernails) shows Great Uncle Raymond and Great Aunt Rose something on his phone. Auntie G dutifully pays attention while Uncle David explains his timetables.

My family. The people I love more than anything in the whole wide world.

All at once, I know why I left my Rachel-Bailey dress at home. "Wait here," I say. "And try not to worry."

Before I can change my mind, I hurry up the garden, into the house and up the stairs to the spare room.

The room – my room – is bathed in rose-colored light.

The sunset pours through the gappy curtains and across the bedspread, skimming the tops of the shopping bags still jumbled on the threadbare floor. A shimmering pink sheen drenches the cans and jars and boxes and the piggy bank on the dressing table. Even the buttons glimmer and gleam in an almost-pretty way. But the light glows brightest of all in the mirror on the wardrobe door.

The wardrobe. Where Mizzy the Marvelous's mystery first began.

I smile. What a mystery it was. Muddled and messy and all sorts of topsy-turvy, just like me. I got it wrong. Then right. Then wrong again. But even though the policeman thought we were all mad, I know I solved the case.

Great Aunt Jane would be proud.

Actually, I'm pretty proud of myself.

Kneeling down by the bed, I lift the edge of the bedspread, peek underneath and grope in the dusty dark. I hold my breath and try not to think about spiders. Until, one by one, my fingers find Great Aunt Jane's diaries.

I pull them all out. Wipe the dust off the covers with the arm of my hoodie. Then, checking the dates on the front of each book, I stack them in a towering pile, with June 1973 on the top.

I lean back on my heels and smile. Everyone thought Great Aunt Jane was just an interfering busybody, snooping around after the Batts and Belfrys of St. Jude's Junction. But she didn't let that stop her. She didn't care what anybody else thought.

I reach for the top book, flip open the cover and flick to the last page of writing. Well, not writing exactly. Little grooves and lines, shaded all around like a leaf print.

I run my fingers across Great Aunt Jane's ghost words.

Then I scoop up every single diary, lock them all in the wardrobe again, and slip the key back in the piggy bank. Some skeletons really should stay in their closets.

Uncle Lionel's eyes flash white in the twilight, as I run back down the garden. "What did they say? When you told them? What did Mum . . ."

I cut him off. "Nobody said anything because I didn't tell them. I put the diaries back in the wardrobe."

The sun sinks behind Auntie G's wonky-wig roof. A bat zigzags through the gloom. A breeze ruffles and clatters the poppy heads.

Oli gapes at me. "Now I really don't understand."

I shrug. Neither do I. But my tummy knows it's the right thing to do.

"But, Miz, don't you want the others to know how brilliant you've been?" says Oli.

I smile and shake my head. I know I'm Mizzy the Marvelous. Oli and Uncle Lionel seem to sort of know it too. So what if nobody else does? My marvelousness can be the new family secret.

"Oh, Mizzy." Uncle Lionel pulls me into a rugby-playing-bear-crossed-with-a-mountain hug. "Thank you. Mum would have been so upset . . ." When he finally lets me go, he reaches into the pocket of his baggy pants – down, down, down – and pulls out a brown-paper parcel. "Here." He smiles shyly. "This is for you."

My tummy fizzes. I snatch the parcel, fumble off the string and rip the paper apart. And there, cradled in my hands, is my very own Hunza hat.

My heart swells. Finally. It isn't pristine white, like I've always imagined it would be. But it's perfect. A sort of soft pinky brown. *Small potatoes,* Pip-Squeaks would call it. Somehow, it feels just right.

I pull the hat onto my head. "What do you think?"

Uncle Lionel tips his head one way. He tips it the other. Then he grins and wraps me in another hug. "You look marvelous, Mizzy. Marvelous."

"Yeah, Miz," Oli adds. "Very cool."

My heart melts. *Very cool.* That's enough.

For now.

GRATE ANT JANEZ NOT-A-MURDA
HOW I SOLVD IT
BY MIZZY THE MAHVELLUS (DETEKTIV)

ME

1) UNKEL LIYONELL IS MABELZ SUN
2) GRANMA MABEL GAVE GAJ COFF SIRRUP TO MAK HER SLEEPEE SO SHE WOODNT TELL HER SEECRIT
3) UNKEL LIYONELL PUT POPPEE SEEDS IN GRANMA MABELZ GLAHSS COZ HE WOZ MAD SHE GAV HIM AWAY

BUTT

4) GAJ AND GRANMA MABEL SWOPPT RUMZ

SO

5) COFF SIRRUP + POPPEE SEEDS = GAJ DED (BUT NOBODEE REALLY KILLD HER)

# Author's Note

Thank you so much for reading *A Skeleton in the Closet*.

I am forever grateful to all of you who helped me create Mizzy. Like a patchwork quilt, she is a little bit of every person with Down syndrome I've had the pleasure to work with (and learn from) over the years. Threads of India and Rose, a whole swathe of Isabela and snippets of so many children who I wish I had the space to mention here.

For thirty years I've wanted to give you all a hero who looks like you. The hero you deserve.

For everything I got wrong, I apologize. Like Mizzy, I'm still learning.

For everything I got right, may Mizzy's story, like her investigations, nudge us to dig a little deeper.

To see the possibilities beneath the stereotypes.

To never underestimate anyone.

Especially ourselves.

# Acknowledgments

So many thank yous (more than I've probably managed to remember, so please forgive me if you're missing from the list) . . .

To Mum, for typing into the night and showing me what was possible. For cheering me on through my own attempts and, for the last few years of your life, believing I was already published.

To Dad, for all the hours of Beatrix Potter and Mary Plain and for showing me that a day spent reading is never wasted.

To Paul S . . . what can I say? No matter how massive my meltdowns, you always tell me it's completely understandable. I'm completely understandable. Your heart just keeps getting bigger.

To Atti, for coming along and reminding me that of course I should be writing for kids, then using up any available time. Seriously, though, thank you: I am who I am because of you.

To Papa Lorne, for taking us in and giving us the home by the sea in which I always dreamed of writing (and for being one of Mizzy's very first readers).

To Luna, for the encouraging ankle licks and the miles and miles of plot-walking.

To Emma, for taking over from Mum as Mizzy's number one fangirl and for being as excited as I am to celebrate every step of her publishing journey. You are the best sister I could ever want (even if you did keep putting me in cardboard boxes).

To Paul H, for making up so many stories with me in our childhood (especially the epics involving small plastic horses, birthing foals in midnight thunderstorms).

To my nieces and nephews . . . Abbey, for being the first child to crawl inside my heart and make the space your own. Joe, Finn and Oli for letting me smush you into two brothers, instead of three. And Bailey, for always asking how my books are going and sharing your own writing.

To my Canadian cheerleaders, Jeanie, Jill, Corinne, Zuzu, Karli, Joe and Leslie, and to all the dog walkers of Gonzales Beach (not to mention the dogs). Your patience and interest and enthusiasm means more than you might ever know.

To SLJ, for sending me off to Canada to "write that novel." Not quite Margaret Atwood like you asked for, but here it is.

To the Daffies, for four decades of love and laughter (and crumpets with Red Leicester cheese).

To Angela Angelillo, whose wisdom and patience has picked me up and put me back together so many times over the years. One day I'm using your name in a book.

To Amy Thrall Flynn, for being the first to make me feel I could actually do this writing thing. And to the one and only Chloe Seager, who glimpsed Mizzy's potential and scooped us both up under your soaring wings.

To my Mizzily-marvelous editors, Lucy Courtenay and Lynne Missen. One person who gets me would be amazing, but two? I'm thoroughly spoiled. And to everyone else at Farshore and Tundra for putting up with my endless questions and suggestions and making my Mizzy dreams come true.

To Binnie, for bringing Mizzy to life. Your artwork is beyond perfect. And to Lester: your family tree is so much better than mine.

To Heidi Crowter and Madison Tevlin, for recognizing Mizzy and giving me the go ahead to share her.

To my lovely network of published, just published and about-to-be published kidlit authors for your patience and generosity and inspiration. Your world is a wonderful place to belong.

And last but very much not least, my MG debut buddy Philippa Leathley. I could not have survived the last nine months without you.